The Devil Takes a Holiday

The Devil Takes a Holiday

Lisanne Valente

Copyright © 2020 Lisanne Valente

The moral right of the author has been asserted.

Apart from any fair dealing for the purposes of research or private study, or criticism or review, as permitted under the Copyright, Designs and Patents Act 1988, this publication may only be reproduced, stored or transmitted, in any form or by any means, with the prior permission in writing of the publishers, or in the case of reprographic reproduction in accordance with the terms of licences issued by the Copyright Licensing Agency. Enquiries concerning reproduction outside those terms should be sent to the publishers.

This is a work of fiction. Names, characters, businesses, places, events and incidents are either the products of the author's imagination or used in a fictitious manner. Any resemblance to actual persons, living or dead, or actual events is purely coincidental.

Matador
9 Priory Business Park,
Wistow Road, Kibworth Beauchamp,
Leicestershire. LE8 0RX
Tel: 0116 279 2299
Email: books@troubador.co.uk
Web: www.troubador.co.uk/matador
Twitter: @matadorbooks

ISBN 978 1838593 049

British Library Cataloguing in Publication Data.
A catalogue record for this book is available from the British Library.

Printed and bound by CPI Group (UK) Ltd, Croydon, CR0 4YY
Typeset in 11pt Adobe Jenson Pro by Troubador Publishing Ltd, Leicester, UK

Matador is an imprint of Troubador Publishing Ltd

For my Big Brother
Harry Bocker
Thank you for being my friend forever

With Thanks To

My wonderful husband, Paul
My sons Paul-Mark, Christopher and Michael
My beautiful DiL Hayley
Your encouragement and support
Makes it all possible

My Brother
Harry Bocker
You made this happen

Dave Hill for bringing my characters to life
You made them all real
My friend and favourite artist

Lorne Maclaine of Lochbuie
For all your advice about Castle Moy
Your clan and the clans on the Isle of Mull

My good friend Diana Gabaldon
For your guidance, reassurance and help
In all matters.

One

If ever there was a time in my eternal life when I became dissatisfied, I would have to say that time came after the Mistdreaming War.

The three mistdreamers chosen by the archangels – in all their glorious wisdom – were a plague upon my kingdom, and had wreaked havoc upon my kings, presidents and demons since their very inception.

However, as I sit on my throne today, tapping my nails on the black marble armrest, the sound bounces from one blackened wall to the other. The only other noise I hear is the hissing and spitting of coals as they turn red for a second when the sound reaches them.

I need to take a moment to calm my temper and take stock of all that has happened to get me to this point of intense fury.

Many angels did not fare well in the Thousand-Year Angelic War, in some respect. Personally, I achieved much and gained even more. When the war ended, the remaining seven archangels took it upon themselves to expel those angels whom they deemed to be the cause of the long struggle.

As they were thrown out, the seven locked the gates to Heaven and then watched my people cross into my kingdom. I welcomed them. They are my children. How dare those smug, patronising, supercilious angels, lord it over my family? How dare they think my family were no longer suitable for Heaven? They had fought bravely and those who survived should have been forgiven. But, no, my brother (the archangel Michael) swoops in with his sword and decrees – yes, decrees – that they who opposed his army should be disposed of and discarded.

But, to make matters worse, two archangels – the holier-than-thou Ambriel and Omniel – decided the time was right to secretly create and then introduce mistdreamers: their own personal spies.

The first set of mistdreamers emerged in the seventeenth century; they were like annoying bugs. A quick swipe, and the bugs are gone. But not so the mistdreamers. No quick swipe was successful there; instead, they bred like rats – begetting family upon family of mistdreamers – until, eventually, the 'cousins' came into the world. The cousins who would cause destruction in my kingdom. These are descendants of the original mistdreamers; those same irritatingly interfering humans who can cross between realms and listen to conversations on matters – and let's be honest here – that have absolutely nothing to do with them! To top it all, they then have the utter gall to relate said conversations to the absolute antithesis of my existence – those archangels who caused my family to be removed from Heaven – leading them into my kingdom!

No, they didn't just throw out my family – my fledgling demons – they also evicted my kings, princes, presidents, dukes and all of my rulers, one of whom is Flauros, my closest ally. My friend. My marshal. Ha! He who cannot tell a lie if he is standing in a spelled triangle. He who was my representative in the Mistdreaming War, had assured me that the troublemaking warmongering loser known as Prince Lucias has vanished. Prince Lucias is the hybrid demon son of my most trusted adviser, King Balam, and the witch Angela, she was the same human who mated with a mistdreamer, produced one of the interfering, nosy cousins and then had the audacity to believe she was good enough for my realm. I am told the witch is dead, and of course my friend Balam killed at the hands of one of the bloody mistdreamers!

I can feel my blood boil again, so I must take time to myself, breathe evenly, smell the sulphur and relax before Flauros arrives.

I check again that my spelled triangles are in place, hidden from Flauros's view on my marble floor.

I do so love my throne room, with its walls of anthracite, which glow red every now and then as they spit and hiss in the intense heat. The darkness suits me, especially given my mood today. As the Conjurer, I have spelled several areas on my black-and-white marble floor. It was almost fun doing it, knowing that Flauros will be uncertain of what to expect.

He's late, as usual.

I tap my long fingernails on the black marble armrest; I'm not happy. The beasts who are embedded in the throne are picking up my energy and writhe in time to my heavy breathing. Their debauchery flows like a primitive rhythmical dance, with their bodies twisting and turning, stretching over one another and moving onto whatever body they can impale. Normally, listening to their moaning, and their screams of pain and fear eases my mind, but not today. Today, I'm infuriated.

Where the hell is Flauros?

"Sire, you called for me?" And there he is, standing before me, slap bang in the middle of one of my triangles; the fool.

I wave a finger at my babies, and the squirming bodies cease all their activity. Their eyes are wide open in wicked anticipation.

"You decided to honour me with your presence then, Flauros? Should I be grateful you found your way to my throne room eventually?" I ask.

I laugh to myself because I can see all kinds of internal battles going on in his mind. He opens his mouth to speak, and I know before he says anything that he intends to lie.

He frowns, as he's just realised that he's been caught out. The magical tendrils have wrapped themselves around his legs, and he can no longer move. "I… I… I…" he stutters.

The game is getting boring now, I just want to hear what went wrong. "I… I… I…" I mimic him. "What are you trying to tell me, Flauros?" I say, then I thrust my head forwards, glaring, as he attempts retreat, but the tentacles hold him steadfast. "You wouldn't be trying to lie to me would you, my friend?"

"Of course not, master," he whispers angrily.

"What, then, do you have to tell me about the Mistdreaming War?" I wait to hear that which I already know, but I look forward to seeing Flauros bleat.

"You probably know everything already, master," he says acerbically.

"My, my, you are pushing the boundaries of our relationship, don't you think, Flauros?" I say, sinisterly.

Flauros retracts immediately, apprehensive that he may have overstepped the mark.

"How about we start again," I suggest menacingly, "Just for the moment, let's pretend that I'm your king, your master and your all-powerful controller." I take a moment to regain composure, as my temper is fraying at the edges. "Let's just say that I've not heard anything about the Mistdreaming War, that

I don't know of my young demons being destroyed, and that…" I breathe slowly, regaining control, but it's too late; my face is in his and I'm screaming at him, "That stupid, mistdreaming halfbreed Lucias isn't on the run!"

Flauros tries to recoil from me, but it's not possible; he shudders fearfully. "My apologies, sire; I've been taking an inventory of all the losses as well as those who have not returned."

I rise and walk around my throne, clenching and unclenching my hands. I don't want to hit Flauros, but I have now gone beyond the point of me simply harming him, and have reached the point where I can imagine him in one of my dungeons, chained to the wall, whilst one of my demons – class two, preferably – is having fun with a cattle prod, as I happily watch him being tortured!

"How can I put this into words you will understand, Flauros?" I sigh and look at the trembling duke. "I don't want an inventory; I want information on why it was possible that thousands of my demons — the best-trained demons — were killed by three puny girls. Can you answer me that or is this beyond the realms of your capability?"

Flauros waits until I, the Conjurer, am once again sitting on my massive throne before responding. "Firstly, sire," he begins – irritated that I could think the mistdreamers were puny, instead of the very capable spy-come-assassins that they were – "they are not puny girls. They are mistdreamers and have been walking amongst us, in our kingdom, for many years. I believe not even you were aware of their presence in this kingdom?"

I roll my neck, as the crick that is developing is causing me some discomfort, tension and stress. Who would have believed that I – the Devil – could become stressed, caused by these girls' treachery? That doesn't excuse the fact that no one – not a demon, a king, a duke nor I – had any idea we were being spied upon by these mistdreamers. I wait to hear more from Flauros.

"I know what you're thinking, sire," he continues, holding his hand up to prevent me interrupting, "You are wondering how nobody was aware of their presence. Well, I say to you that there were those who knew and conspired against all of us, and they were those to whom you gave your greatest trust."

Mentally, I envisage choking the life out of him, and I'm gladdened to see his hand shoot to his throat. Flauros grasps at his neck desperately. Pain is shooting through him like a thunderbolt as I twist and turn his larynx with the simple movement of my index finger, crushing the life from him, and then, by my good graces, I choose to let go of him. He gasps in, taking a long breath and rubs his neck, his body limp.

"Do you know where that damned George Lucas got the idea of his Darth Vader's tricks, Flauros?"

Flauros shakes his head, completely bewildered; some sense of reality returns and he manages to shake his head. Anxiety crosses his face, as he's distressed and unsure of where this strange turn of discussion is heading.

"Yes, nod your head," I command. "I realise you're incapable of speech just now, as I almost crushed your larynx, but you'll be able to talk in a few minutes. Anyway, back to George; good, old George, stealer of ideas. It was I who placed the thought into his head. Do you honestly believe any mortal could think of something as devious without my help?"

"I have no idea who this Darth Vader is, sire," Flauros croaks, "Is he one of the minions on level one?"

"Are you mocking me?" I shout.

Flauros draws back, certain that there will be another assault, and prepares for the agony. Almost pleadingly, he insists,

"Most definitely not, sire. I will seek him out and bring him to you so that you may punish him as you see fit. First, though…"

He looks at me with completely perplexed eyes, and I try not to laugh; at least he's making me feel a little better.

He continues, "Would you be so kind as to tell me where I may find him, because it is a name unknown to me?"

"He's not real, you imbecile!" I swear I'm dealing with the stupidest of beings. "He's a figment of the imagination of a director of movies. Movies made on Earth. I'm trying to share the information with you that…" I'm aggrieved, again. "It wasn't a figment of his imagination, but of mine. It is I who gave him the idea of Darth Vader, but do I get the credit?"

"Um… no?"

"Do I get the thanks?"

"Erm…"

I storm towards him, but this time he's prepared for the assault, so I change my mind and instead I touch his face gently. How much pleasure is it to watch terror change to confusion? It's one of my favourite things, unlike whiskers on kittens!

"Sire?" Flauros asks quietly. He is perplexed, but alarmingly fascinated by the petulance of his master, half expecting his master to stamp his feet like a spoilt toddler!

I have strayed into my own mind and become entangled in my thoughts, which are steering me away from the very purpose of this conversation.

"Enough of this," I insist and look around my room, which has suddenly lost its appeal. My love for this is no longer intoxicating but is strangling me.

Flauros is completely confused by the change in my demeanour, wanting to ask what was bothering me, his master, but afraid of the reaction. He stands still, waiting for the next outburst. "You've had enough," he ventures eventually, "of your throne room?"

The first Flauros is aware of my displeasure is the smell of rancid flesh seeping into his nostrils. The foul, revolting odour makes him reach to his face, and cover his nose and mouth. It is permeating his skin; there is no escape. He attempts to take a step back, but the invisible, magical tendrils hold him still. His eyes close as he wrinkles his face in distaste, and he exhales disgustedly. When he opens his eyes, the horror of me, his master, peering directly into his eyes, almost crumbles his sanity with fear.

My eyes had seeped black, when he'd asked me that ludicrous question. I mean, enough was enough.

As Flauros is hit by the odour of Hell, I force my head in towards his face and wait until he opens his eyes.

Ah, terror; it takes my own breath away at times, and I enjoy the moment, almost retreating until I remember his foolish question. I allow the horrors of all the depths in Hell to be seen through my eyes, including areas in my kingdom he had never been aware of. There was no need, after all, for him to go beyond the three tiers to the fire pits and dungeons, as he was a great duke with thirty-six legions. Had he discovered a situation in the lower levels that needed to be dealt with, he would have simply consigned one of his lowly servants to discover the problem then report back.

Flauros sees beyond infinity and crosses into the depths of despair until, finally, visions of himself appear. All manner of evil, together with trials he would have to endure, are laid plainly before him. All reason leaves Flauros as he stares into the dark abyss in my eyes, and he searches for any traces of himself in the black pits.

He begins to think quickly of how he might remove my rancour, but all ideas evade him. He could discuss the Mistdreaming War, but it is sure to make a bad situation even worse. If he speaks of Darth Vader, he will surely explode, and any trace left of him will be sent to hidden places from which he would never be rescued, nor would any of his demons even care to find him, due to being too busy with improving their own lot in Hell to consider anything else.

"Erm… I can see a stupendous imagination, sire, one that is definitely not of a lowly human and…" he rushes to finish, my eyes widening with each word, "one which has not benefitted from the glory it so deserves"

His words work, as I withdraw my face and return to my throne, with my body leaning against the armrest, but it is clear I am still dissatisfied, as – when I retreated – I growled at Flauros, who turned his head away meekly.

I laugh quietly to myself as I see Flauros take a deep breath, relieved he can no longer see the visions I had put forth for his benefit.

"I do not want to incur your wrath again, master, but, for your benefit, perhaps we should discuss the Mistdreaming War again?" Flauros suggests.

I flick my fingers in his direction and nod my head, which should be enough for him to continue with this exercise. I know he cannot lie, so I await the report patiently.

He explains, "We were winning the battle at Mingary Castle, but the witches had placed powerful spells around the keep; ones we could not penetrate. So, we called the angels from the castle to the land outside the keep. It was magnificent. The ground rolled and turned, spewing up all that is evil in the earth thanks to the enchantment the witch Angela had placed upon the ground—"

"Wait," I interrupt, "you took Lucias's mother with you; whose brilliant idea was that?" There was no need for a reply, but I wanted to hear it from his mouth; I knew it had been the idiot Lucias, who had used his mother once more.

"She proved useful, on this occasion; her spelling of the ground worked, many angels were lost, some dragons and the repulsive fae—"

"You managed to destroy angels, dragons and fae, yet no mistdreamers?"

"Sadly, no; when the ground began to suck them under, they removed themselves from the area. All, that is, except the one."

"And why did she remain?"

I watch as Flauros's face turns red; he's angry and rightly so.

"Lucias kidnapped the child of Mairi," he explains, "She remained and searched for her baby, and was able to return to the castle before my demons could capture her."

I can feel my blood boil; I grunt and roll my eyes, and my neck clicks as I rock my head from side to side. "And then… continue," I command. I wait and hear more.

"We rested that night, but, when daylight came, we were unaware the angels and mistdreamers had left the castle," Flauros confirms.

"So your magnificent witch knew nothing either?"

"Lucias cut her head off."

I close my eyes in despair, and a squeal slips through my closed lips. I can feel my heart beating rapidly, with frustration and fury building to a rapid tempo. My head begins to pound and my face crumples as the squeal turns into a magnificent screech. It bounces from wall to wall, which spark red as the noise penetrates the coals.

Flauros cowers before me, but continues to ramble. "I swear we were winning, my lord, until we were called to Glencoe."

I take deep breaths and puff them out through my mouth, making my heartbeat slow down. "Glencoe, please tell me about Glencoe," I insist.

"Well…" he pulls back, watching me carefully, expecting a strike of some form or other. "We were outdone by a brilliant strategy."

"Would this be like the brilliant strategy of the First Mistdreaming War? Or the brilliant strategy of the Dragon War? You remember them don't you, Flauros? The first being when my friend King Balam was killed and his murdering son, Lucias, prevailed upon himself to kidnap the mistdreamers, but didn't kill them! And the second war when he escaped with the help of the angel Paschar."

"We couldn't have won that, sire; it was futile. The dragons and fae outnumbered us, and Lucias had his strategy completely wrong; we were lucky to escape with our lives at all!"

I'm just too tired to listen to any more, but still he bleats on.

"Whereas, at Glencoe, the fae and angels worked together like a Roman platoon—"

"Much the same way as they did in the first war," I interrupt.

"That's correct, yes, but this time we were bombarded by the dragons and…" Flauros stops; he doesn't want to say any more.

"Don't stop there, please continue and enlighten me as to how legions of demons, demon kings, and minions were beaten," I plead sardonically.

"It was the erratics that ended it for us."

"Big stones?" I query wearily.

"Yes, erratics. Erm… They changed into the MacDonalds, who were massacred in 1692."

Once again, Flauros finds himself looking into black eyes, with my face nose to nose with his. Through the depths of despair, he can see himself chained and beaten.

"Get out," I hiss. "Get out before I send you to my version of 'never-Neverland', and it's not a place Wendy will come to free you."

I push him with one hand and his body explodes; parts of him fly through the walls and will connect in another part of my kingdom, and I have sent other parts to my dungeons, where they will remain until I free him.

I have to visit Earth and right this wrong done to my people.

Two

The archangels Omniel and Ambriel were scrutinising the planet Earth through the Heavenly Glass, which is a massive, dome-shaped magnifying glass sitting in a round table etched with the names of countries and hieroglyphics, Inserted all around the table are discs, which are the Keys of Earth. There are blue, red, green and yellow buttons, one for each country; when pressed, each one gives out information about regions, languages, people of import and immediate concerns, depending upon the colour of button pressed.

Just then, one of the blue buttons over Scotland was flashing again.

"Here we go again, Omniel. I thought that, with the last war, Scotland would go through a period of rest," explained Ambriel.

Omniel laughed. "You worry too much; Scotland always has a flashing blue light around it. I blame the black pudding, personally!"

"This is not a joke," Ambriel said seriously, "There is something amiss."

Omniel tried to conceal his amusement, but his silvery blue eyes danced merrily.

"What..." Ambriel said grumpily, "What is it you're not telling me, you... you angel, you?"

"Harsh words." Omniel coughed, hiding the laugh that threatened to erupt. "What I can tell you is that I received a message from one of the mistdreamers."

Ambriel was surprised that one of the mistdreamers had contacted Omniel, but, after the Mistdreaming War, they had begun to trust him more. They no longer viewed him as the all-powerful archangel, but more as a trusted adviser and friend.

"Which mistdreamer would come to you before speaking with me?" Ambriel asked curiously.

"It wasn't so much a mistdreamer as one of their guardians," clarified Omniel.

"Omniel," Ambriel shouted in frustration, "how many times have you to be told to leave the mistdreamer's children alone, and let Xaphan and Adramelechk do their jobs?"

Omniel had the good grace to look abashed, and his face turned a fiery red. Taking on the manner of the superior angel, he began to speak, but, before he had the opportunity, Ambriel held his hand up in the age old sign of 'don't go there!' Rather than acting upon his very ruffled feathers, Omniel looked down. Ambriel was right; he should leave the children alone, but he suffered from the loss of their mother and father: the mistdreamer Mairi and the angel Appoloin. He was positive Ambriel was like him in that Ambriel blamed himself for their deaths.

"You have the right of it, Ambriel; I should stay as far from them as possible, but have you seen them lately?" he queried excitedly. "They're growing so quickly, and Xaphan has them taking part in daily exercises with their wooden swords."

"Every day?" asked Ambriel surprised, "Are they not a little young for that?"

"That's what I thought when I heard, but they are thriving; in fact, only yesterday—"

"Yesterday?" Ambriel screeched.

"You know," Omniel said huffing, "you shriek like a witch when you lose your temper; it's so very un-angel-like. You need to get a grip."

"Get a grip?"

"And there you go again, repeating every word I say. Are you not understanding my words? Do you feel it necessary to repeat them?"

Ambriel counted each and every one of his deep breaths before responding, whispering his words as though in prayer, "God give me strength!"

"Shall we start again, Omniel?" Under his breath he murmured, "Oh great one," before turning away, just as Omniel raised his eyebrows. "Why were you with the mistdreaming children yesterday and why do feel the necessity to constantly check up on them? Do you not trust Adramelechk and Xaphan to do their jobs?" He held up his hand again as Omniel began to splutter, "Jobs that you specifically asked of them."

"I did, but—" began Omniel.

"You did, but you still feel the need to interfere."

Omniel blustered; he knew he was on shaky ground with Ambriel, but it was his right after all. Wasn't he the superior archangel? Wasn't he supposed to ensure the safety of man and especially the little mistdreamers? His eyes softened at the thought of the little boys.

"And there you go again." Ambriel interrupted Omniel's thoughts. "They're little boys, who will grow to be good men with the support and protection of those whom we put in place to protect and guard them."

"I just needed to see how they were getting along, and to know that they were coping," explained Omniel.

"No, you just wanted to see them." Ambriel smiled. "I can find no flaw in that; they are amazing little men: half-angel and half-mistdreamer." He waited until he knew Omniel was listening, then continued, "But we must step back, Omniel, and let them become the gifted humans they will be, without interference from us."

Omniel, fairly chastised, bowed his head and nodded. "You have it right, Ambriel – I know you do – but I feel such pain in the loss of Appoloin and Mairi; I blame myself and wish that I could change the past. My only saviour is visiting those little boys; they give me hope, when I thought there was none."

Ambriel put his arm around the sorrowful archangel, and walked him towards the Heavenly Glass. "We have this to watch over the whole world, Omniel, not just the mistdreamers. I know you feel guilty, we all do. But, in fact, it is not our fault; it is that of Lucias and all the other demons, who worked against, not only us, but also against the Dragon and Fae in their desperate attempt to eliminate mistdreamers."

Omniel snapped his fingers. "We have digressed from our purpose here, have we not?"

Ambriel was surprised by the sudden change in conversation and waited for his friend to continue.

"The mistdreamer Valerie visited me, from her home on Tír na nÔg; she had news of our brother Lucifer," Omniel explained.

Ambriel rolled his eyes. "Oh no, what's he done now? Could he not just stay in his kingdom and enjoy what he has – what he wanted?"

"It would appear that our brother has decided to go to Earth and change the past."

Ambriel's eyes flew open. "But he can't… we can't…" He drew a breath and continued, "How does he hope to achieve this?"

"I don't have all the details, but I know he is furious with Lucias, and I expect he is plotting to change the outcome of the Mistdreaming War in Glencoe. If that is the case, I have a plan, and we need to use the Heavenly Glass to put it in place."

Ambriel began wringing his hands together. "This is really why you visit the children, is it not? You fear for their lives, and, ultimately, you can assist them more than Xaphan and Adramelechk."

Omniel raised his arms, his hands waving in denial. "No, not at all; I trust them implicitly. It is my failures that make me visit the children. It is my own guilt and not anything other than that. I do not believe I could protect them any better than Adramelechk or train them to a higher degree than Xaphan. He was the best warrior we had, and it hurt him sorely when we believed he was traitorous and had crossed over to Lucifer's side. Luckily, he was acting on our behalf, or who knows what would have happened."

Ambriel smiled. "We have Michael, and he trained Xaphan, so I think we would have managed."

"True, true," Omniel replied, nodding his head, "but I would never have underestimated Xaphan's prowess."

The two archangels remained silent, both lost in their own memories and thoughts as they gazed down upon the Earth through their Heavenly Glass. The lights embedded in the table surrounding the glass flashed on and off periodically, indicating trouble or problems in different areas of the globe. A war here, a tornado there and somewhere the ice cap was melting – the light was on constantly, and this area was of major concern. A bomb exploding and another shooting. At that time, the world seemed to be in a state of flux; it was never calm. Lucifer travelling to Earth could only disrupt any level of harmony they hoped Earth would eventually achieve. As the lights around the table flickered on and off, archangels Omniel and Ambriel gazed down upon the Earth.

"So what's the plan?" asked Ambriel.

*

I, Lucifer, find myself striding up and down my black-and-white marble floor. I have changed into the form of a human because I know the sound of my hooves echoing in the throne room will give me an even bigger headache than the one Flauros has left me with, and I find it easier to walk purposefully whilst on human feet.

I stretch my legs and touch my horns; I know if I am to go to Earth, it can only be in human form. I can feel my blood boiling again. If I go to Earth, I have to right the wrongs of so many of those whom I have placed in positions of power and trust in my kingdom.

What does that say about what I think of them? It's contempt, pure and simple. I abhor every single one of them just now. They've led me to this situation – this tenuous position wherein I have to sort out the problems they've caused.

And it's just not fair!

I want to get away from all of them and from all of this. I sweep my hand around the room, but I don't mean I want to get away from this room. It's a welcoming place, even though the bodies writhing in my throne have ceased, being unsure of what is going on. I can feel their displeasure, and I'm not sure if it's with me or the fact they are no longer carrying out their incessant licentious acts. I will assume it's the latter because if it's the former, I intend to burn the throne with them in it!

My heart is pounding, my eyes are misting and my nerves are jangling, and I feel as though my whole body may burst into flames – again.

Anger is an understatement.

I gaze at myself in the mirror. The horns have to go. I run my hands slowly around them, and they disappear. My bestial face has to change, or I'll frighten the people on Earth. I wave my right hand down my face, and my beautiful beast goes. In its place, I can see I still have the golden eyes of a feral cat. I wave my left hand from left to right, and they are changed to a warm, deep brown, and are almond shaped, with long, dark eyelashes.

My eyebrows are arched and shaped, and my nose is straight and longish, not the button nose of a pig. My mouth is wide, with generous lips covering large, white teeth.

I have no hair!

I touch my head gently, and hair begins to sprout; I watch as it grows. I don't want it too short, so I let the dark-brown waves fall to the nape of my neck.

I am beautiful; perfect, in truth.

What's next? Yes, my body has to change; it's too powerful when in the form of my beloved beast, so I alter my torso – making it not too slim and not too muscle-bound – and lengthen it to the appropriate size that will suit my long legs.

I am standing naked, admiring my physique, but something is missing: the penis. Why they want these ridiculous dangling objects always baffles me, but they serve a purpose, I suppose.

I swipe my hand at my groin area and I'm impressed with the magnificent monster I have created. Perhaps it's a little too long, so I go to shorten it, but I change my mind. The human-male psyche has already taken hold of my brain! So I leave my mighty prince as he is, thick and long.

The mirror gives a 360° view, I can see my well-defined backside, and my powerful thighs and calves. I have a strong chest with a sprinkling of black hair, wide shoulders and muscular arms. I'm slim with a tight stomach. I am delighted with my work. Now I need to dress.

I choose Armani; it's what you have to wear, isn't it? Who could resist? I fix the bow tie and pull down my dinner jacket; it's exquisite. Then I remember I will be going to seventeenth-century Scotland, and they've never heard of Armani, and definitely won't appreciate the cut and style of this beautiful suit.

I refuse to wear a kilt and I know if I dress like the British, I'll be stabbed before I take my first step. So, trews it is, plus a Highlander shirt with leather ties, brogues and leggings. I throw a woollen cape around my shoulders and line the inside with fur.

I think I'm dazzling; who could resist me?

I am in a much better mood, the headache has lifted, my nerves are jangling with anticipation instead of my earlier fury, and my throne has returned to its continuous writhing; I can hear moans of sexual bliss emanating from the wood, so absorbed in their dance of perversions are they that they are unaware that their screams of passion are no longer silent. My children revel in my pleasure.

I wave adieu and, with a flourish, I release my wings. My beautiful, massive, black wings that stretch six feet above my head are resplendent with magnificent, shiny feathers. They stretch, opening wide, and I lose my balance for a moment; it's been such a long time since I've had the need to use them, that I've almost forgotten the power they hold.

A breeze floats under them, and they lift me off my feet. I look upwards, and, with the sound of clanging cymbals, my wings soon have me soaring above the gates of my kingdom.

I hover for a moment and, with a laugh, I look to Heaven, pull my wings back and dive towards Earth.

I am going on a holiday!!

Three

"So what's your plan?" Ambriel asked again.

Omniel took a deep breath, closing his eyes and focussing internally. He raised his head to the heavens and allowed his marvellous white wings to sprout from his shoulders. It was a wonder to behold, and the heavens remained still as they shared in the enchanting celestisl tinkling of bells, as Omniel opened his wings.

Ambriel acknowledged the marvel closing his eyes in appreciation and with a slight upwards quirk to his lips. "Beautiful, Omniel," he said, "but you still haven't answered the question."

Omniel returned to the subject at hand and shook off the warmth of serenity to address the question. "What's my plan? I'll tell you, Ambriel. We will await Lucifer's fall to Earth and we will bespell him."

Ambriel slapped his head in frustration. "Oh no; we cannot return to the witches. You know they'll be most displeased if we ask them to aid us again. They're only now living in some peace."

Omniel jerked back in surprise. "We need no witch to help bespell Lucifer; we have the power within ourselves. It's up to the witches if they want to continue with the spell whilst he remains within their vicinity. Our casting will last for the month and no longer."

"Are you sure of this?" Ambriel asked.

"Most definitely! Why should we allow his venture to go smoothly? Why he's probably already allowing his vanity to take precedence over reason."

Ambriel chuckled. "I think you'll be right in that. How do you suggest we should continue?"

"I am sure he would be aware of a spell being cast; he is always attuned to any dark magic, but – and here's the kick – he's never aware of angel glitter. He's turned his back on the goodness that it can bring. I say we sprinkle him as he falls."

Ambriel touched his chin, listening to his friend with interest and nodding along with the words.

"He'll be so engrossed," Omniel continued, "in falling and destroying mistdreamers that he won't notice."

Ambriel was aghast. "Do you think he intends to seek out the mistdreamers and end them?"

"I have no doubt that, if he could find them, he would cause a great deal of trouble, but with the safeguards so firmly in place around the whole mistdreaming family, it's difficult for us to even find them. We only know of their location because we helped enforce the safeguards. Even our Father is unaware of exactly where we have secreted them, and He prefers to not know."

Ambriel looked doubtful. "I find it strange that our Father, being omniscient and omnipresent knows not where they are."

"Let us just leave that for the time being, Ambriel; personally, I'd rather believe He wishes to remain outwith the mistdreamers, business, choosing to let them carry on their work without His interference."

"Hmm," Ambriel grumped, "or it's an easy way of not having to deal with trouble."

Omniel wanted to disagree – to defend their Father – but, in truth, their Father was shirking a lot these days, and Omniel was certain He was now indifferent to His mortal project, having moved on to another one, allowing humans to make their own mistakes.

"It's no wonder so many humans have turned from Him," stated Ambriel.

"What do you mean, Ambriel? Surely they don't blame Him for their own foibles?" Omniel queried.

"I don't think they blame Him; I am of the opinion that they just don't believe He exists, and who can blame them for their points of view? Their world is in a catastrophic mess and their understanding of the all-powerful, loving Father is that He wouldn't allow any harm to befall them."

"You cannot be serious! Even if they brought the harm upon themselves? He is not a sweeper; He does not clean up others' messes, which they have caused."

"You and I know this, but we're talking about humans. You remember that stubborn, independent race who were given free will and chose to use it as is their right?"

Omniel sighed; this was turning into an angelic political discussion, and he would rather leave this alone. They could argue and try to work this out for a millennia, and humans still would not have faith or take responsibility for their own mistakes. "I can understand that they would like help whenever Mother Nature has had to bear down upon the Earth. It turns into an earthly disaster and, of course, innocent lives are lost from their world. They perhaps see the disaster as one that could have been prevented by our Father, and that the innocent and weak are those being punished. What humans don't seem to realise is that we had already assigned those humans to leave that plane, long before Mother Nature changed some aspects of the land."

Ambriel was deep in thought; Omniel's words were reassuring, but he could also understand the stance of the humans. Not where they had caused conflict and blamed his Father for the outcome – no, that was purely a human fault – but when natural disasters occurred, he felt his Father could have intervened, and the loss of any human life filled him with sadness.

"We digress, Omniel," declared Ambriel. "We are supposed to be discussing how we can prevent an ungodly interference with the natural progression of the Earth, following the Mistdreaming War!"

"I know, I know," Omniel agreed reluctantly, "I get a little overbearing when it comes to the political side, do I not?"

Ambriel wanted to agree, but knew – by the look on his friend's face – that if he did, it would only cause him pain. Instead, rather than lie, he reintroduced the subject of Lucifer, guiding Omniel back to the plan he had insinuated he thought would be a good idea. "So, you believe if we sprinkle angel glitter it will affect Lucifer."

Omniel smiled; he was pleased to leave politics to one side and deal with something for which he could at least ensure the outcome.

"I suggest when we see our brother Lucifer falling… and I mean falling to Earth because, surely, there are no further depths to which he can descend?"

"Only he knows, Omniel; after all, it was he who created Hell. I have no idea how far those depths are… and, to be honest, I have no need of that knowledge."

Omniel shuddered. "Some of our Infidelibus brothers will have first-hand knowledge, including Xaphan; no wonder he is so protective of the mistdreaming children."

Ambriel smothered a laugh, not because of Xaphan or the mistdreamers, but rather because it appeared that Omniel was on another branch of the conversation, yet again. "Omniel…"

"Yes, yes, yes; the angel glitter and our brother Lucifer."

"If we could get back to that, brother, it would help, and time is passing. We know that when Lucifer sets his mind to something – as you said – he doesn't think, but merely goes into action, so the quicker we set about this plan, the better prepared we will be for the eventualities."

Omniel nodded in agreement. "Right, right, of course. What I said earlier. We will cast the angel glitter over the Earth's atmosphere, so he cannot avoid going through the magic."

"What do you intend to include in this spell of yours?"

"Not just mine, Ambriel; you are an accomplice to this also."

Ambriel rolled his eyes; his brother could never stand taking on a duty that he might have need to question. At least if Ambriel was included, he would tell their Father just that: that he was party to the fact! "Go on, before you babble away at something completely outwith our conversation, what are you including in the spell?"

Omniel jerked his head; frowning, he answered crossly, "I do not babble; I give coherent advice."

"And there you go, babbling again." Ambriel looked around the room for a seat. The seats were clouds: large, fluffy, comfortable clouds, sitting on a floor of blue sky. The walls were a cornflower blue, whereas the ceiling was the dark, deep shades of a purple sky, littered with tiny stars, which cast their light upon the room and twinkled to the sounds of the angels' breaths.

Ambriel threw himself onto one of the clouds and sunk deep into its comfort. Putting his fingers together in an arch, he tapped his forefingers in a steady motion, awaiting Omniel either completing his plan or giving another lecture.

"And I can read your mind," Omniel interjected.

With a wave of Omniel's hand, Ambriel found himself sitting on the floor, with the comfortable cloud-chair having disappeared to God only knew where! "There was no need to do that," he moaned, "I was just waiting to hear the rest of your plan."

"You were being disrespectful, brother." Omniel laughed, a booming sound that sent the stars into a frenzy. "Oh cripes." He screwed up his face as he watched the stars dancing merrily. "Earth will be waiting for a meteor shower now and when it doesn't happen all sorts of theories will be put forward as to why the phenomenon of the 'jumping stars' happened."

Ambriel smiled despite himself. "You really have to learn to control your laughter; it wreaks havoc with all the world when you lose it. It's not quite as bad as the tempests you cause in your fury, but look at the stars – they're still in disco mode!"

Omniel slapped a hand across his face to prevent another raucous roar.

"And don't think them up there don't know you're still laughing; they can feel the merriment, and we shouldn't be merry at all, because we have mistdreamers to protect," scolded Ambriel.

"And humans," added Omniel.

"Mistdreamers are human…"

"They're just a bit more."

"Yes, they are."

"I suggest we cover the Earth's atmosphere with angel glitter." Omniel surprised Ambriel by returning to their original conversation. "This magic will send him out of time to when he wishes to go and it will send him in another direction also."

"That doesn't sound too bad; at least we'll have time to get other areas prepared for whatever it is he's planning in the month that he will be spelled. Now wait…" Ambriel was a bit confused. "If he goes into a different time in one month and then manages to leave that time to go to another month, does that mean the month we're giving him becomes null?"

"No," Omniel assured him. "The month we give him starts with us from the time he goes through the Earth's atmosphere; he can go to any time in BC or AD, including the future or whenever, but the month will still be in place."

A worry line appeared on Ambriel's perfect forehead. "Unless someone alters the timeline?"

Omniel grew impatient. "That goes without saying; thankfully, there are relatively few on Earth with that capability."

"Perfect." Ambriel clapped.

"There's another thing: I've added a little surprise for him; he won't like it one little bit, but it serves him right for being such a devious, arrogant, vain, self—"

Ambriel cautioned Omniel, and urged him to stop by using the classic palm-out hand gesture. "I get the picture; he's not the best of fallen angels. What is it you've included that will be 'extra'?"

Omniel shook his head, and his wings rang merrily as his body moved. "Let us just sit back and watch; it's something you don't need to be an accomplice to, and if there is any fallout, you can remain completely innocent."

Ambriel was drawn suddenly to the Heavenly Glass; a black dot had appeared in the sky below them. It looked harmless, but if it was on the mirror, it was a warning sign. Sure enough, before he had the opportunity to say anything to Omniel, every button on the table surrounding the magnifying glass began to flash.

Omniel raised his hands, his wings stretching to their full width. Ambriel, on recognising what was happening, unfolded his wings. They stretched out and touched Omniel's, and, as they met, they began to sway in harmony. The stars in the sky became quiet, their radiant lights dimming to the danger surrounding the Earth.

Ambriel kept his eyes on the Heavenly Glass, not losing sight of the blackness creeping towards the Earth. When Omniel began to chant, Ambriel joined with him after the first few words, adding his voice to the spell being cast.

When the blackness closed in towards the atmosphere, Omniel stopped the incantation and blew. As the air left his lips, it floated downwards, with a trail of sparkling glitter following his breath. The glitter spread across the whole Earth, encasing it in magic, just as the blackness entered the atmosphere.

The darkness spiralled out of control, spinning and twisting in every direction; the lights and buttons on the Heavenly Glass's table flashed and beeped, screaming for help across the world.

Then all went silent, only the moon shone on the black mass, which lay in a heap on the ground – without a head.

Four

My head is killing me!

I had no idea that falling through the Earth's gravity would cause me, the Prince of Darkness, to suffer from a human ailment. I need to clear my head and work out what happened on my descent to this planet.

I remember most of my journey to Earth. I'd not long finished dressing, I had been concerned that wearing a tie might be too much and had changed into Scottish regalia. I left leather ties at the neck of my Jacobean, white shirt loose, allowing just a few dark chest hairs (enough to titillate the females) to show. I'd taken one last look at myself, and the only word that came to mind was 'sexy'. Oh, 'hot' and 'exquisite' were there too, but I was damn sexy; they wouldn't be able to resist me here.

After admiring myself, I incanted – remembering to include the date and place of where I wanted to arrive – then, raising my wings, I flew towards the Earth.

I find it peculiar that I was pulled into a vortex when I entered the atmosphere. I somehow managed to get a modicum of control, but, by then, I was so tired that I can't even remember landing on the ground. I must have passed out; I – the Prince of Darkness – fainted. Now isn't that a turn up for the books? And one that won't ever get printed in any one of them, because if ever it does appear in print and should anyone find out, there won't be a demon left alive to tell any tales.

I passed out, and here I am now with this thumping headache, and all I want to do is find the accursed Laird MacIain of the Glencoe MacDonalds, right the wrong the mistdreamers did to my kingdom, and get the hell away from this planet.

My holiday has not begun the way I intended.

I was planning a quick entry, job done, no need to mingle with the peasants, do a bit of 'fraternising' with the ladies and then get back to my throne room. I'm now in disbelief. What was I thinking about when I decided to come here? Why do I always act irrationally? It's one of the reasons I was 'removed' from Heaven, but that's a story for another time.

I stand, and these legs wobble – they didn't do that in my throne room – and I nearly fall down again. What has happened to me?

Looking around, all I can see are the dark outlines of what must be trees and ferns. However, I can hear the ebb and flow of water, but the sight eludes me under the darkness of the night. Even the stars have dwindled; their lights are dim in the purple sky. The only light is the moon. It shines on a building in the distance, which is the only one in the area that I can see, and so, with shaky steps, I start moving towards it.

The air is fresh, and the soft, cold wind blows through my hair, winding loose strands across my forehead; its soft touch gently rids me of the dastardly headache. With each step I take, my legs become stronger and better acquainted with the terrain. I walk through fields of soaking-wet ferns, even the slightest touch from them makes my skin crawl. I'm wet, I'm cold, and the area below my chest is causing pain; it feels empty. Good grief – I'm hungry. I'm tired! As I walk more, my eyes begin to close; could this get any worse?

Eventually, after a mile of walking, I hear the sound of voices. Two girls or women are chattering; I don't understand their language, but they're laughing, and that's a good sign. If I ask them what building I'm approaching and the best way to enter it, there's every possibility this night might end better than the way it started.

I see them. One looks to be about fourteen the other is perhaps in her twenties; it's difficult to assign an age to them as their bodies are hidden beneath the heavy, shapeless, long dresses and capes they're wearing.

"Excuse me, ladies," I say in my most alluring voice, "perhaps you could give me some help; I appear to be lost."

Both ladies stop their conversation and turn from each other to look at me. Their faces fall, their mouths drop open and – instead of the happy, carefree young women they were moments ago – they, at first sight of me, become women in abject terror.

Now it's my turn to be shocked as they scream in horror and run from me faster than a couple of gazelles being chased by a pack of lions.

"What the hell?" I say to myself as I watch the retreating forms of the ladies vanish quickly.

Did the entry into the atmosphere cause my beauty to be altered? I can deal with that when I see what the problem is, but I'm truly concerned.

My steps get heavier and heavier as I approach the building. In this dark light, it appears to be dark grey and in the shape of a rectangle. It's difficult to note exactly what it is, because it is surrounded by trees, and all I can see is the top half of the building above them. It has two turrets to the right side, and I'm delighted to realise it must be a castle; I like the crenellations around the parapet. It should, however, have a man guarding it, not just a fire!

When did Glencoe build a castle?

Why am I walking and not using some of my magic?

I am surprised to find that I am standing at the base of the castle. By the looks of it, the magnificent castle has been built upon a volcanic rock. I was right: it's a giant rectangle. I walk around it to find the entry. Three of the walls are just protection, but the wall to the rear, which is hidden in a tangle of branches and bushes, has a small door with two steps down to it.

Just as I begin to walk down the steps, the door opens and a short man – well, one who's shorter than my height of 6 feet 2 inches – stands before me in tartan trews and a tartan waistcoat. He puffs out his strong chest, pulls back his wide shoulders and stands like a sentinel before me, preventing my entrance into the castle.

I take a closer look at him; his eyes are piercingly blue and his age, like the girls before, is difficult to decipher because of his ruddy cheeks and white beard. They like to hide their age do these Scottish humans.

I put on my best smile and take another step forwards.

"Aye, ye'll stay where ye are, man; ah'm no' lettin' ye intae ma castle, no' just yet," declares the man.

"I promise you that I am not here to cause you any pain, Laird MacIain," I lie.

"Whit're ye talkin' aboot, man? Ah'm nae the MacIain; he's a' Mingary Castle. This is Moy. Dinnae tell me yer lordship finds himsel' loast." The man chuckled. "Ah wudnae hae believed it."

Now I'm completely baffled; what's going on? "You're not the MacIain of Glencoe?" I ask reasonably, dreading the answer.

"Glencoe? Away an' come in, man; ye're far aff the beaten track. Yer naewhere near Glencoe."

"You're not the MacIain?"

"Ye'll find that every clan chief is a MacIain. It's no' their name; it's a title. Ah'm Laird MacLaine; ah'm no' the clan chief, so ah'm no' a MacIain!"

I can feel my headache returning; why have they got to be so damn awkward in this country?

I take a step into the castle, grateful for the little warmth within. He is obviously a miserable miser, as the place is lacking in heating, carpets, any kind of comforts appear to missing. Instead, he's strewn hay and petals across the floor.

"Do you have no carpets here?" I ask somewhat reasonably.

"Carpets, in the main hall?" He is astounded, "Why wud we use guid thread tae hae it walked upon by dirty feet? Naw, ye'll no' see any 'carpets' here. There are some rugs in the sleeping chambers."

"And fires, do you have them?" I question, shivering in my wet clothing.

"Aye, we hae fires: peat-burning fires that we put oot at night tae save money. There's no need tae waste it; we can get warm in oor beds." He lights a couple of candles and places them in the wall sconces.

They give some light to the room; not much, but at least I can see where I am standing. We are in the great hall, as he would call it, which has long tables either side of the room, with wooden benches, and a stone floor covered in fresh hay with heather and petals scattered atop, giving the room a pleasant smell. The tables are polished to a high sheen.

I look up; the ceiling isn't as high as I expect, but that will be to keep the warmth in the room. A circular, wooden candle holder hangs from the centre of the ceiling, with at least ten candles in place. All of them are unlit. At the far end stands a massive fireplace with dwindling embers; yet, in my state of chill, I can feel the warmth from the embers from twenty feet away and so I make my way towards the heat.

"Aye," says the laird, "ye'll be missin' the heat where ye come frae."

Now that stops me in my tracks. Slowly, I turn to face him, my eyes narrowed. I begin to take in the stock of the man. He has a sharp, intelligent face, and his eyes watch me, untrusting and disbelieving. I can see he's waiting for me to make a mistake. "Do you have a bottle we could share and perhaps discuss a few things?" I query.

"Ye'll no' be bleedin' me dry o' any o' ma drink," he blusters.

"It never even crossed my mind; all I wish for is for us to learn about one another over a civil, decent glass of whisky."

"Ye'll find a jug an' two cups in the corner there." He points to the far corner, beside the fireplace. "Ye'll no' see me turnin' ma back on ye; no' until the deal ye want is set."

I step slowly to the corner, lift the jug and cups, place them on the table nearest the fireplace, and sit with my back to the warmth – what little there is. I'm shivering, so, with a twist of my forefinger, I raise the flames in the fire and I feel myself relaxing almost immediately.

"Ye'll be replacin' that peat yer usin' an' aw." He glowers. "We're no' made o' money, ye ken"?

"I think you have a lot more money than you're sharing with me, probably stashed under your bed or stuck in a wall somewhere," I posit.

He watches me slyly, and a sardonic smile crosses his face. "Ah kent ye'd ken where ma money wud be; it'll be safe or ye'll find yersel' in the cellar."

I throw my head back and laugh out loud. "Have you any idea to whom you speak?"

The laird crossed the room and sat opposite me, placing one hand on my wrist and gripping it so tightly I thought he would break one of these human bones, as they're so fragile!

"Ye'll listen tae me, Nick, an' listen tae me guid. Ah'll allow ye tae remain in ma keep, but, in that time, ye'll no' play any trickery upon me or ma staff, and ye'll keep yer thievin' mitts to yersel'."

I have to admit to being very impressed. Here is a man who is definitely in charge, but never would be of me. However, I need a place to stay; I have to find my bearings before settling the mistdreamers' debt and moving on.

"Why do you call me 'Nick'? Do you know who I am?" I ask, surprised by his intuition.

He picks up the jug and pours a liberal quantity of the amber nectar into the two empty cups before handing one to me. I lift the cup and place it to my lips, keenly observing him over the rim. His eyes are looking down at the cup, they close as he takes a sup, and then he opens them suddenly, staring right back at me. He'd known all along I was watching him. He is definitely one to have on my side.

"Aye, ah ken who ye are," he confirms.

"Enlighten me," I say intimidatingly.

"Ye're the Deil."

I smile and nod my head.

"Whit ah dinnae ken is whether ye are here tae save us or end us. If it's the former, ye're welcome tae stay; if it's the latter, ah'll be throwin' ye in oor secret cellar masel'."

Now this is where an incredible change happens to me: I actually tell the truth. "I cannot believe I am about to say this, for it is the truth."

"Ah'm listening," he counters.

"I have not made my mind up yet, and for the foreseeable future I see no reason to harm anyone in this place; I need a base for my business and this suits me well. It's clean," I say, pointing to the fresh rushes and flowers on the floor, "tidy, hospitable and – by all manner of means and up to a point – friendly."

"Aye, well, ah wudnae push the friendly part too soon," he says, then stands and walks away. "Ye'll let me ken when ye've made yer mind up, aye. An' whilst yer here, ah hae a boon tae ask o' ye, should ye stay."

"What would that be?"

"My brother is tae ken ah hae a powerful guest an' that ah'll no' be takin' any mair o' his nonsense, are we understood?"

I look to the fire and take a small sip from the cup, letting the warmth of the whisky drip slowly down into my chest, heating me from within. I shrug. "It's a simple request, and I can grant that, yes."

I watch him walk away and, for the life of me, I cannot understand why I want him to stay; it's almost as though I'm enjoying his company. "I have a question though, if you could perhaps help."

He turns and looks at me scornfully, breathing deeply as if it were all too boring to meet the Devil and have to speak with him. "Go ahead, name yer request; if ah kin help, ah'll try."

"It's not a difficult one, really; I just require a little help in choosing a name for myself, to use whilst on this plane."

"Ye mean whilst yer here, ye shud get rid o' aw that fancy talk, else folks'll think yer saft in the heid."

There are so many things to remember, and I doubt one will stick in my head, which is still thumping like the drums of Hell.

"What about Joe Black?" I ask hopefully.

The laird starts walking back to me and I'm pleased we will continue this conversation. "Ye cannae call yersel' that," he states.

"Why not?" I ask back, feeling affronted; I thought it was a great name.

"Why it's the name o' the soul collector, death himsel'. Ye call yersel' that an' naebody will speak tae ye. Dae ye no' ken the name o' yer ane folk?"

"I have more than one soul collector, and you've got to remember that the other side have their own collectors also. He might be from their side."

The laird draws himself to his full height and chuckles, then, with a little disdain, he whispers under his breath, "It's a shame it's nae you who cannae lie when in a magicked stane."

I'm taken aback, impressed and also more than a little suspicious. "How is it you know so much about my world, and yet I know nothing about this place?"

"We like tae keep oor ane company on this island; we can keep oor battles small an' easily handled wi'oot ootside forces. We survive on the fruits o' oor ane labour an' rarely leave the island. Why would you, in yer fancy kingdom, even care aboot a wee land like this? Yer too busy interferin' wi' all yon on the mainland tae hae a care frae us."

"Aptly put and quite right," I agree, but he has piqued my interest. "This island isn't far from the mainland, though, is it? You can cross, can you not?"

"Ye hae tae go tae Tobermory an' get a fisherman tae tak ye tae the mainland."

I scratch my head; all his advice is swirling around in my mind. "We haven't come up with a name for me yet; have you any ideas?"

"It's an easy one that, Nick – 'cause yer Auld Nick, are ye no'? An' Mahoun."

"Wonderful, that's settled then: I'll be Nick Mahoun. Lord Nicholas de Mahoun. The 'Lord' adds a little dignity to the name, don't you think?" I sup a little more of the delicious whisky, pleased that I have discovered the perfect name for myself.

"Ye'll get some funny looks when ye tell folk yer name, but they'll ken tae gie ye a wide berth if need be. 'Lord' is an English term, so it'll no gie ye much dignity up in the Highlands, that's for sure." he laughs and walks away. Over his shoulder, he calls to me, "Come, catch up, yer lordship; we shud be addressing yer other affliction."

"What other affliction?" I ask through my happy whisky haze.

"Ye dinnae ken," he roars with laughter. "Come wi' me tae the lookin' glass an' see."

I'm beginning to sober already, and move beside him.

"Here tak a look at yer bonnie face in the looking glass." He actually laughs so hard, he begins to cough and can't catch his breath. He falls forwards, slapping his knees.

It is funny to watch, and I smile, then I turn to look at my face.

There is nothing there. If I had a face, it would have drained of blood and turned white. If I had a head, my hair would be standing on end. If I had a neck, the blood vessels would be standing out like wandering tree branches.

"The bastards!" I yell.

Five

After my initial shock upon learning that I have no head, I curse the angels – and I know who they are: my darling brothers Ambriel and Omniel. They will be the ones to have ruined my life; they always have and will continue to do so until the end of time. However, having rested in a very comfortable bed, I have to admit that – after a generous breakfast to sop up the large amount of whisky I downed late last night – I am content, though this is a feeling I'm not used to. So, I take my leave of MacLaine for the time being, and head towards the stable.

I didn't take a minute to look at myself in the mirror; if I am going to terrorise those on this island as the Headless Horseman of Moy, so be it; I'll enjoy watching them run in fear – they should be terrified of me!

The serving wench this morning actually flirted with me; she is the same lass I met on the way to the castle, so I'm guessing the old laird is a witch and has somehow cast an enchantment on his staff to see my face. That suits me fine, until I have time to take leave of them.

I have chosen a black stallion for my ride to Tobermory. He's a beauty, but I am under threat of death if anything should befall the laird's favourite beast. He is quite magnificent, and I sense he is one with me as he struts and shakes his mane, prancing around the castle keep.

When we at last make our way to the road, I find it's barely a beaten track, even though it is the main thoroughfare on the island.

I whip the horse to go faster, he rises to the occasion and has me flying with the wind at our backs. I have time to look at my surroundings: trees everywhere, rolling hills and a loch to the north of the castle, which is now in the far distance and hidden by the trees. I realise that will be my saviour; nobody knows of the place, so I will be safe and hidden in the castle whilst I prepare my plan of action.

A memory of the loch flits through my mind, but it passes so quickly that I let it fly away with the annoying midges of this land. Surely they have to be tiny demons escaped from my kingdom and if they are, I'll make sure they work for me or will return them from whence they came.

I ride further north, and there is a break in the landscape where I can see another castle. This must be the Duart Castle, which belongs to the laird's brother.

They have had a series of battles; MacLaine supports the British, and his brother supports the Stuarts. Their relationship is so fraught that MacLaine even changed the way his name is spelled: no longer is it MacLean. I laugh to myself; this is definitely something I can use to my advantage and I will work with it. If they remain head to head with each other, then one will want me on their side, and I will provide the assistance they need – for a price. And I know many humans are prepared to sell their souls to me. Joe Black – aka Azrael, the angel of death or the collector of souls – ha! He's not in my league.

When I reach Duart Castle, I hold the horse for a moment at its entrance, unsure if I should venture in. My hesitation leads me to believe that now is not the right time to make an enemy of MacLaine or a friend of MacLean. I have other business that must be attended to before I sort out this family to my benefit.

I am surprised that I can feel again. My only perception for several millennia has been anger or betrayal, and yet, now, I have this weird sensation creeping into my belly. One that makes me want to laugh, not sing – no, never sing – I think it's called joy. It's such an odd feeling, and one I'm not sure I like, yet my heart and soul are rejoicing with the pleasure of freedom.

I am happy; the Prince of Darkness is actually happy.

*

I knew that feeling wouldn't last long, but last it did, all the way to Tobermory. When I arrive in the little town, I first see to the horse's needs. He is a magnificent beast, and the whole journey had been superb thanks to his pace and power. It had been a pleasure to ride him; subsequently, I leave him in a field of the greenest grass with stables with the freshest hay, and I know he is already looking forward to our return journey. It's been so long since he had such a horseman as me on his back.

Having checked he was secure and resting comfortably, I contemplate my next move as I gaze across the Sound of Mull to Ardnamurchan. Tobermory Bay, with its colourful houses, rounds the pier to one side, whilst boats and yachts are anchored in the dock.

I take a short walk to the pier and I meet with a fisherman, and, before long, I am embroiled in another situation.

I ask the fisherman if he will take me to the mainland, but he tells me, in no uncertain terms, "No". He claims the water is too turbulent, yet, when I check it, the ripples are small and steady; there's not a choppy wave in sight. There's certainly nothing so wild that would prevent the crossing, merely whitecaps bobbing gently on the water.

He, however, refuses steadfastly to take me across the Sound to Mingary, claiming the water is changeable. I am now reduced to having to use my power, even though I know it is better that I don't. If I use it, I will become more visible to the powers that be, who are those very super-beings I am trying to elude, in order to enjoy my first holiday from Hell.

I cannot fathom the fisherman's reasons for being so obtuse and then, of course, realisation dawns – he's Scottish, and I have yet to meet a more arbitrary, stubborn race. He's just refusing me for the sake of it.

I offer him another incentive: gold.

He's not interested.

Scratching the beard that has appeared on my face since I last shaved, four hours ago, I have a brilliant idea. "What about I buy your boat?"

"An' how will ah mak a livin', if ah dinnae hae a boat tae fish?" he asks in response.

"With the amount I'm prepared to give you, you won't need to fish again, and… after I've been to my destination – and returned – you can keep the boat."

"Och, I'm no' sure," he says, his dour face screwing up as the sun breaks through the clouds. He takes a peek skyward and, after reassuring himself, with a disgruntled, "Hmph," he agrees to take me over. "Aye, for the price o' ma boat, an' ye'll pay noo or ye'll be tossed in tae yon water." His head dips slightly in the direction of the sound, just in case I'm not sure what he means.

"Then let us get on our way, my man," I say, and even I know that sounds pompous.

But the fisherman just shakes his head at me, curling his lips. "Aye, that'll be when ye've paid me."

I pull the leather pouch from beneath the cape the laird kindly had given me, and squirrel out several coins. I'm surprised to notice his eyes widen when I drop them into his hand.

"You thought I lied, didn't you?" I ask, a little frustrated by his obstinance.

"Of course ah did; yer Nick Mahoun, are ye no'?" he asks whilst unwrapping the length of rope from the harbour post. Then he jumps into his boat and waits for me to do the same.

"I am Lord Nicholas de Mahoun, yes; have we met before?" I say, surprised, as I toil to get into the vessel without landing on my back. How easy he made it appear.

"Ye dae ken whit 'Mahoun' means in the Highlands, aye?" he enquires as he presses his oar into the harbour wall and pushes the boat off towards the river.

I wrap the cloak around me, pulling it tight into my body as I sit on the bench facing the fisherman and the way we are heading. "I'm sure you'll be only too willing to tell me, so please enlighten me."

"Mahoun, means the Deil, in auld Scots, so it wisnae hard tae ken who ye are when yer name is the Deil's callin.'"

I chuckle to myself; that canny old laird knew that. I am most impressed. Better than that, I know the joke will be reciprocated, but I doubt he'll enjoy the consequences. "So I'm the Devil, am I?" I query, certain he will lie.

"Yer uncanny handsome for the Deil, but then ye'd hae tae be, wudnae ye?"

"Why do you say that? Surely if I were the Devil, I'd have a forked tongue and horns, and walk around on hooved feet."

"Ah've nae doubt ye dae when yer in yer ane abode." The fisherman squints over his shoulder to see how far we've crossed and seems relieved that we have nearly arrived. He shudders at the thought of having to take me, the demon, back to his town, but he has made a deal and he can't break the promise, now that the bond has been paid.

"Good answer, Mr Fisherman; you could easily have lied."

"Ah figure there's nae point in lyin' tae ye; it surely wud mark ma soul, which is already crowded wi' sin, an' another will just tak me even nearer tae spendin' ma eternal life in yer kingdom. If ah can help masel', then ah ken ah'll hae tae change ma ways. There's nae better time than the noo tae start."

"Are you that afraid of eternal damnation? Do you not think that being with me might be more fun than playing with angels all day?"

"Och, ah'm no' afeard o' eternal damnation, an' playin' wi' angels might be deadly dull, but it'll beat the punishments ye'll deal oot tae the lost souls. Ah'm no' very guid when it comes tae pain, ye ken?"

I'm about to launch into the 'we don't always hurt; sometimes we just have fun' speech, but I don't get the opportunity, as the man jumps from the boat and wades to the edge of the land, pulling me and the boat closer, in order that I don't have to step into the water.

"Ah'll be takin' the boat a ways downstream; ah'm thinkin' yer no' wantin' the MacIain tae see ye, is that right?" enquires the fisherman.

My ears prick up. "The MacIain of Glencoe?" I ask.

"Whit? Ye mean the MacDonald, the one who was massacred? No, Nick Mahoun, ye'll no' find him bidin' here; ah believe he's wi' his wife an' sons, playin' wi' the angels. Ye shud hae done yer homework afore comin' here, naw?" He chuckles and begins pulling the boat.

I am aghast at his cheek, but even more impressed with his strength as he tugs and yanks the boat into place, then covers it with fallen branches, topping them with clumps of moss.

"Ah'll be right here waitin'," he says, and crawls under the branches.

I stand watching as he disappears under his makeshift hideaway, and am a little dazed. Then, realising I had better move, because the sky has turned grey and I don't want to give the fisherman the opportunity to deny my chance of return, I call upon my powers and cloak myself in a glamour that will keep me hidden from mortal view.

Plodding through dense forest growth, I walk for about a mile, hiding behind large trees in case I am being followed. It's very unusual for me to feel jittery, but I have to admit – as I walk through the undergrowth and push my way through soaking ferns – I have the ominous feeling of being watched. Whenever the chance arises, I hide and I'm not ashamed to admit it because, after all, I'm on a mission as well as a holiday, but still a presence hovers around me.

I shake away my uneasiness the minute I hear it: a child's laughter.

I know Mingary Castle is nearby and there must be many children under the protection of the laird, but, still, there is a special quality to the child's voice. It's almost angelic, I think, as I walk into a clearing and stop still in my tracks, near a flower bush.

Two beautiful children are at play, sword fighting. Their bodies are identical: they're the same height, they have the same sturdy legs, and their little arms already have signs of muscles. Their skin is weather-beaten and golden. One, however, has wavy, dark hair and eyes as green as emeralds, and the other one has hair so blond it is almost white and, unlike the other, his eyes are as blue as a summer sky. The likeness is undeniable. Their lips are shaped like Cupid's bow, and they have little, pert noses, they are stunning children.

Angelic, I think.

Their legs hold them still as they slam each other's swords, with tremendous force for five-year-olds, yet neither one is falling or losing balance.

Their hypnotic, carefully choreographed sword play holds me mesmerised. Each boy knows exactly where to land the sword, with speed and perfect timing, so they know how to prevent themselves being stuck or touched.

So lost in their magical play am I that I don't notice the little blond one turning his attention towards the forest. I duck straight away when I realise where he is looking and try to work out the distance from the bush to the forest and whether I would have enough time to make it to cover, unseen, before they become aware of me.

That is when I notice the two men. How have I not seen them before? They stand like silent stone sentinels, and it is obvious, by their stance and every nuance of their bodies, that they are the boys' guardians. I recognise the traitor Xaphan, his long, wild hair blowing freely in the wind. His body armour covering his muscular frame is more akin to that of a gladiator than an eighteenth-century Scottish warrior. He is wearing steel armbands on his forearms; his stomach is visible, with its perfectly asymmetric muscles; and a silver strap hangs across his chest, from his shoulder to his waist.

Here is a fallen angel who has sat at my table and given me his allegiance, and then acted as a spy for the group of assassins they call the Infidelibus, who are those angels chosen to guard the mistdreamers and act as their guides.

If there is one angel I will kill and ensure his soul ends up in the dead zone, it will be Xaphan. I will enjoy every moment of watching him die.

Beside him stands the enormous, muscle-bound fallen angel Adramelechk. His blond hair is tied back at the nape of his neck with a leather thong. He searches the area for danger to the children constantly.

I had heard he blamed himself for the deaths of the children's mother, Mairi, and their father, the waste-of-space angel Appoloin; perhaps that is why he is so fearful for the little boys.

I have to watch, as the interaction between the angels and the boys is fascinating. The little blond boy is 'stabbing' Xaphan regularly, who feigns injury every time, which has the child squealing with glee. The dark-haired boy holds Adramelechk's hand and giggles at his brother's antics. A few times, Adramelechk indicates the dark-haired boy should join in, but he shakes his head in a definite 'no' each time it is suggested; it is obvious he enjoys the fallen angel's company, and vice versa. The only time Adramelechk stop searching the area for threats is when he gazes down at the little boy, ruffles his hair and chats encouragingly to him.

When the blond lifts his sword to swipe at his brother, Adramelechk prevents the toy touching him using a wave of his hand. So, Adramelechk has some of his powers; they're nowhere near the same as mine, but it's definitely something I'll have to remember.

I'm startled when I hear Xaphan howling; he's on the ground. I could maybe make a move and get one of the boys, but then I realise he is only play-acting. The dark-haired one lets go of Adramelechk's hand, pounces on the 'wounded' guardian, and holds him down by sitting on his stomach. The little blond dives across Xaphan's legs, and Xaphan is pretending to be secured by them.

The laughter and merriment is making me quite ill, and I cannot fathom why I'm smiling at the fun going on before my very eyes.

A stocky, kilted man walks out from the castle, calling to the angels. Xaphan grabs the boys, placing one under each of his arms, and strides towards the man. He must be the laird, MacIain of Mingary. He is not dissimilar to my own laird, MacLaine, so I consider the possibility that they might be related, and if that is the case, yet again I have to wonder at the shrewdness of the man; he is definitely one to watch when I put my plan in action.

What plan? What am I to do? The only way I can see to make anything happen is to get hold of one of these magical boys and get them to mistdream me through time, because, as it happens, I cannot for the life of me alter where I am or what time I find myself in.

And I know the sneaky archangels who have done this to me are Ambriel and Omniel: my darling brothers!

Lost in my own thoughts, I do not see the little blond boy pointing in my direction until I hear him shouting, "Look, Xaphan, he's over there."

I can hear Xaphan mumble something, but I can't make out what it is he's saying. However, by the look of the fury on his face, I have an inkling. I glance over just as Adramelechk pulls his sword from the sheath at his back. He too, like Xaphan, is scrutinising all around frantically.

"No, there, Xaphan," squeals the little boy, who is still pinned under Xaphan's arm.

My body turns to ice as I am drawn into the bluest of eyes; they are nearly upon me, searching my soul. It is a sensation I am unacquainted with, and it has my body buzzing like the hives of thousands of bees, all of which are crawling over me. In desperation, I begin to claw at my body, attempting to remove the grip the child has on me.

I watch in horror as his little, fat arm rises and points directly at me. "There he is, Xaphan, right there at the bush. It's the Deil. The mermaids were right: they said he was coming, an' there he is."

My legs are suddenly like lead, but as I watch Adramelechk rush forwards, I run towards where the boat is anchored. I can't run any faster, but I try; these human appendages just don't respond well to command! I move as quickly as is possible, and yet I can hear the pounding on the ground as Adramelechk chases me. He cannot see me, which is to my benefit, but he catches the movement of the leaves as I brush past them. The speed with which he pounds the ground as he runs in my direction almost matches the thumping of my heart.

I race to the boat, and my fisherman has removed the camouflage of branches that kept him hidden, thankfully. With a flick of my hand, my glamour vanishes, and he sees me coming rapidly at him. "Get ready to move," I shout, "Get moving!"

As he pushes away from the edge, I jump into the boat, and pull my cloak tightly around my head and body; first, I crouch and then I lie upon the floor. The fisherman's strong arms pull and scull powerfully, and we are half way across the Sound before I begin to breathe easily.

"Ah wudnae come up yet, Nick: the angel is still watchin' for ye across the water."

"How do you know he's an angel?" I ask, surprised.

"The same way ah ken ye're the Deil."

And that was the end of our conversation until he bade me farewell at the Tobermory pier on the Isle of Mull.

Six

The Mermaids' Tale

A question often asked is this: "Where do mermaids and fairies come from?"

To get the correct answer, you have to return to the very beginning, and it's a long, complicated history; I apologise for the lecture, but if you want to know, then it is written so for any future research you may have to do!

All changes relevant to this tale begin with the Thousand-Year Angelic War. When it ended, the seven archangels closed the gates to Heaven. They watched the remainder of the angels who had sided with Lucifer – at least, those who had survived the war – walk away from paradise to their new kingdom. As they walked towards the gates to Hell, their bodies began to transform with each step they took. By the time they had reached the gates, their angelic bodies had transformed from an ethereal light into large, bestial subhumans.

The war had raised many concerns amongst the angels, and the Council of Angels was formed. The committee comprises representatives from the three spheres of angels, and within each sphere there are three tiers of different types of angel.

The first sphere encompasses seraphim, angels with six fiery wings; cherubim, who have six white wings and powerful heads; and throne angels, the ones who listen to the Father and resemble older men, but have the most radiant wings.

The second sphere contains the dominions, the virtues and the powers. The dominions are similar in appearance to breathtakingly beautiful humans. They have enormous, white, feathery wings. The virtues are strong, celestial and spiritual, and miracles are performed through them. The powers look like strong, strapping warriors and wear full armour, including helmets. They carry shields and weapons; they keep their swords and spears always by their sides.

The third sphere is made up of the principalities, the archangels and angels. The principalities are senior angels and wear crowns; they carry out orders from the higher level of angels and they pass on blessings to all the worlds. The archangels are the messengers of God and are His first sons. They are very handsome, and their wings are enormous, white and make a sound like the tinkling of bells when they are released. The music from their wings fills the heavens, and the cherubim sing along with the beatific sounds. Angels fall into many different categories within this sphere: there are guardian angels, envoys, messengers and angels who are born specifically to protect the Earth and all the worlds in the universes.

Shortly after the Thousand-Year Angelic War ended, and the council members had been chosen, they held their first meeting. It was one with many positive measures put in place and one that changed the Earth.

They discussed the tedium that had set in amongst some of the sections within the spheres of angels. It was noted that many angels wanted change, as, although none were followers of Lucifer, their equilibrium had been disturbed by the war and they craved something more than their existence. A faction of the principalities wanted the chance to go to Earth and live amongst the human species, to assist them in their lives, and have some control. Another faction wanted to go to Earth, but not be accountable to the principalities; they wanted to roam the seas, not as humans but as another species. The archangels – having the most important role and therefore being the decision makers – agreed, but they thought it imperative that the humans were party to these or any serious changes to circumstances in Heaven, and that some could be of assistance.

The committee agreed that the archangel Ambriel would be responsible for discovering the right humans who would work with them and granted him the gift of mistdreaming to pass on to the chosen people. He was also directed to keep their identities secret and to arrange a council to protect the special humans.

The Council of Angels agreed that half the principalities, with their exquisite beauty, could fall to Earth, taking with them the powers of eternal life, magic, kindness and understanding. They were to work with the humans and learn about them. Their bodies would remain ethereal and glorious. They were introduced to the Earth as the Tuatha de Danann, the children of the goddess Danu. When they met humans, they were smitten. The humans were a completely different race from any they had encountered in Heaven and, in truth, they fell in love with them.

The humans named the principalities the fae and fairies.

The fae made their home on Ireland, but, as is always the case, power, greed, jealousy and ignorance crept into their new lives. They realised the inevitable: that war would erupt. As the fae, they were vastly more powerful than any human, and, in truth, they liked the human race. Therefore, it was decided that, rather than allow the inevitable war to occur, they should move underground.

In a sublevel of the Earth, they created their own universe, Tír na nÔg, which was only accessible to fae and angels. They grew stronger and more powerful in their own world, whilst still keeping a close eye on the Earth and humans, the race who fascinated them.

Four queens were chosen, placed in the four corners of the world and ruled with their kings in what became known as the Seelie Court. When news of an uprising was brought to them – with the aid of a mistdreamer – the Seelie Court was able to expel the troublemakers to the Dark Kingdom and prevent a war, and was eternally grateful to the mistdreamers.

Those disgruntled, warring fae were confined to their new world, and were unable to venture into Tír na nÔg or onto the Earth's land. Because of their choice to cause disharmony on Tír na nÔg, their expulsion meant a change to their appearance. On leaving the fae world, they came to look more like the demons of Hell, but without the double heads; however, they were larger and more powerful.

Within their boundaries, set by the fae, their power was limitless, but only useful in their new world if they had the ability to travel to other worlds and join with other demon races; then the universes would be in real danger.

The new land became the dark seelie world; the strongest – or the one who battled hardest, had more followers and was more devious, unscrupulous and unethical – became the king of the Unseelie Court and ruled over the land. Their land was the antithesis of the seelie world; they didn't have the perpetual sunshine the seelie world enjoyed, but instead they had a glittering ice haven, under a dark-blue, velvet sky, littered with stars.

The Council of Angels agreed that the angels who had chosen to go to Earth and live in the waters, but not be ruled by the principalities, could go. However, there was one law that must be obeyed. The council's decision was that they would be permitted to live in the waters on Earth, but one of the principalities would go with them and become their king. He would be responsible for them and set the rules by which they must abide. He would be entitled to make the laws of the new lands, and if they were broken, it would be up to him to decide how the punishment would be applied.

There was some dissent amongst the water angels, but they came to agreement eventually. When they fell to Earth, they dived into the waters across the world. Upon entering the waters, their angel bodies transformed into those of female humans, but instead of legs they had a long tail covered in iridescent, brightly coloured scales. Their hair was long, reaching to their waists; each of their faces was elfin with large, almond-shaped eyes fringed with long lashes, a button nose and very kissable lips.

The one principality sent alongside the angels dived in and his ethereal body transformed into that of a human male, but, instead of legs, he also had an extremely long tail, covered in blue scales that shone brighter than the stars. His hair was long and white, he still wore the crown of the principalities, and his white beard reached his stomach. Instead of a spear, he held a golden trident. He became King Triton, the ruler of the mermaids.

For many years, they all lived happily. They watched the humans by swimming to the surface and spying on them on the land, making sure that, when they returned to the sea, the humans would only catch sight of a tail.

When humans decided to explore the oceans, the mermaids went into hiding. King Triton built a new world, under the sea, with the aid of his trident. This was a world similar to Tír na nÔg, which was hidden from humans' view and only visible to mermaids, fae and the angels. Many mermaids chose to give up their ocean and live with the king in his new land, rather than face being seen by humans or captured. Some chose to return to Heaven, saddened to leave their watery new life. Eventually, most of the oceans across the world emptied of mermaids. All except a few in Scotland.

King Triton tried to persuade his daughters to come to live with him, but they loved the freedom of the seas, and the depth of the Scottish lochs ensured no human would be able to find them, or not for many centuries anyway.

Three daughters lived in the loch beside Castle Moy, which the locals called 'Linne nam Maighdean-mara' or the 'Waters of the Mermaid'. Like most Highlanders, they were a superstitious breed, believing in the fae and mermaids, and choosing to leave well alone. So long as the mermaids remained in their own world, all would be well.

The three girls were Ailsa, the noble maiden; Aileen, the ray of sunshine; and Annag, the graceful. They often came to the loch's surface and swam to the edge of the loch to lie on the sands, enjoying the sun's warm rays. They were the loch's silkies, and if the locals saw three beautiful girls with tails – a red head, a blonde and one with hair the colour of liquid caramel – then they chose to pretend they were seals!

The final item to be implemented from the first meeting of the Council of Angels was carried out by Ambriel. When Ambriel was chosen to select a group of humans to fulfil the needs of Heaven and Earth, to aid the angels in preventing any further wars and protecting all the worlds, he took many centuries to choose whom he thought would be worthy of the gift. When he encountered the MacDonald clan, he found both men and women to be brave and strong. They were willing to travel, learn and teach, and were more than capable of using their own initiative when necessary.

A sept within the clan, the Park family, were his final choice.

Concerns had arisen in the centuries since the first Council of Angels, and things had become tense. Lucifer's kingdom caused havoc on Earth regularly, and it was believed he would, before long, attempt another war with Heaven. It was imperative that Ambriel install the chosen gifted humans and grant them the gift of mistdreaming, allowing them to walk unseen between worlds.

Ambriel selected guardian angels carefully for the mistdreamers. These angels – who had fallen from Heaven, although they were not part of Lucifer's world – were not quite able to enter Heaven. He hoped that, by giving them this honour, they would prove themselves and be allowed back into Heaven.

They would form the Infidelibus, the guides and guardians to the mistdreamers.

And so the first meeting of the Council of Angels introduced fairies, mermaids and mistdreamers to the world…

Seven
Nathaira Campbell

For a million years, Nathaira Campbell had stilled herself on the seabed. She had watched the comings and goings of Triton's daughters; all of them, she believed, had now passed into his kingdom whilst she remained, lying there like the rocks that surrounded her. When a crab ventured to sit atop her, she allowed her snakelike body to move with the current, toppling it from her person.

She lived on the vegetation found nearby, and, because she moved rarely, there was no need for any excess consumption of food. However, in her motionless state, she had time to contemplate. Where Nathaira is concerned, any deliberating is never a good idea. Whenever she attempted to remember, a white pain seared her brain and it would send her to sleep for another hundred years.

What was her purpose? Why was she still in this place?

She had never been of a kindly disposition, being more amenable to the darker sides of life than the pretty, happy, gloriously beautiful daughters of Triton. They had been tedious in the extreme. Their talk of love and enchantment; their ridiculous treatment of their father when they didn't get their own way; and the brushing of their long hair, fiddling with their nails and always searching above the waters for human males to fall in love with had sent Nathaira into a wretched tedium. Oh how she found them dreadful!

Triton was aware of her, and she knew her place, but more than once she was tempted to spit some venom into the brainless mermaids that flitted and swam around, oblivious to her person.

She sighed. Was this life never to end? Was she damned to an eternal life at the bottom of the sea? Not that she complained, or not much, anyway. Who was there she could complain to: the fishes? They were as brainless as the mermaids.

Her eyelids slid slowly over her hooded, violet eyes. When they were almost closed, she caught sight of a light from the corner of her eye. It was a new life venturing into her space. How interesting, she thought and lay in wait, watching surreptitiously. She would wait patiently to discover who was trespassing into her space and, when the time was right, she would rid the seabed of this new entity that had carelessly wandered so near to her.

But she wasn't to get any peace this day; the ethereal presence made its way nearer to her, whispering with a deep, dark, velvety, baritone voice, "Wake from your slumbers, Nathaira; you are to come to the king's hall."

"Am I to die at last?" she muttered.

"Far from it."

Nathaira opened her eyes and cocked her head to one side. The fish nearby scattered, afraid.

"What is it Triton wants of me, have I not been a loyal subject? Can I not be left to rest?" she asked.

The ghostly sprite weaved like the sea grass, hypnotically flowing to and fro with the movement of the water; it's light shone all around Nathaira, and she was unable to resist watching and unable to return to her rest.

"Don't make me laugh, Nathaira," it whispered. "You are no loyal subject; you were turned into a sea serpent because of your actions towards his daughters. He wants you to make amends now."

Nathaira cast back her memory, and pictures of the past filtered through her mind, but she could find no file that showed her causing harm to Triton or his family.

"I know naught of what you speak, but if Triton wishes to bring me home, I'll come. But not yet; I'll come when I'm ready, not when he wishes," she said venomously.

"I would be careful of how you speak," the entity insisted. "Your king and father wishes you to return… now," he commanded.

Nathaira's body stretched leisurely, enjoying the discomfort she could sense emanating from the sprite. "He has left me to perish and cast me aside, but now he wishes me to return?" she asked sceptically. "Then this is not the same father who sent me to rot, alone, in these waters." She closed her eyes in satisfaction, about to return to her sleep, when she became suddenly alert to the change in the sprite's demeanour.

He laughed at her; why would he do that?

Her eyes flew open and she glared at it. "You have the cheek to laugh at me, in my own home!" She was incredulous.

The sprite continued to sway gently, but she could hear the amusement in his voice when he replied, "Alone? You were never alone, Nathaira. Your sisters were always nearby, but you chose to ignore them and you chose to abandon your family."

"I hardly had a choice," she said dryly, trying to keep the shock from her voice at hearing her sisters had never left. "I'm a sea serpent." Quivering happily and now in control of herself, she added, "And a deadly one at that; just come a little closer and let me prove it to you."

The sprite rose higher in the sea, and Nathaira's eyes followed him as far as was possible.

He declared, "I will return, girl, when I have spoken with the king and I will pass on your response to his commands. Until then, be very careful; treachery is at hand, and he wishes for you to be safe." Then he slipped away with the ripples of the water, taking his light and warmth with him, and leaving Nathaira with an unexpected sensation of loss.

"Get a grip, Nathaira; Father wants me to return," she said quietly to herself, "and that would be a first in thousands of years; why would he wish for my safety suddenly?"

Once she had regained her equilibrium, she would review their conversation and make her own deductions about the reason she had been asked to return to the palace. Her memory was still fractionalised, so the conversation had holes in it the size of those in Swiss cheese; therefore, some of it was a puzzle and one she looked forward to resolving. In a way, that would suit her, not Triton and not her air-headed mermaid sisters. Just her!

She was aware of a second sprite in the vicinity, and she waited for it to make itself known to her, closing her eyes until it spoke.

"You knew I was there all the time," he whispered.

"Aye, what is it you want of me? If it's to reinforce the other one's demands, then you can leave right now. I'm not interested in returning to my father's palace; not yet, anyway," she added.

"Hush, Nathaira," it sighed. "Had I been wanting the same as the other one, I would have shown myself with him."

"You make sense," Nathaira replied, "so then what skulduggery is it you are hoping I will do for you?"

"I will tell you all in due time; he is coming, and we wish you to tempt him."

"Who is coming? I'll not be forced to do anything."

"We wish you to be with us; it is of your own volition, should you choose to do so."

His sinister whispering danced around her head, compelling her to do as he said.

"Do not try to enchant me, spirit," she declared. "I am too old and too wise to fall under your spell. If you wish for my assistance, do not do this by trickery. I will return to the palace with my Father's messenger if you attempt to influence me with magic."

"My sincere apologies," it said reverently. "I was checking to see if you were amenable to listening to our suggestions."

"So there are more of you sprites then, not just you?" she asked.

"We have an army. We want your help to get our master."

Nathaira rolled her eyes; this was beyond stupid. "Do you not see me lying here, unable to move for a million years? You ask me to 'get' your master, but if I move, I will die, and I have no intention of dying, or not yet."

"That's where our magic will help; we can show you how to walk again."

Nathaira's eyes flew open and she saw the sprite watching her with its bright, grey eyes, rimmed with red; its excitement was palpable.

"I'm listening," she said deviously.

Eight

The journey back to the island had been peculiar, with the fisherman refusing any communication with me. I cannot believe it! What did I just witness on the mainland?

Stepping onto terra firma, I turn to wish my fisherman a fare-thee-well, but he has not waited to see if I lived or died, and is already rowing back to the mainland.

I relish the contact with the earth; I'm not a lover of boats or, more specifically, of being in one. No matter the skill of the boatman.

The Scots are truly unaware of the depths their lochs reach. All their scientific equipment has not yet detected the depths of other kingdoms below the seabed. These depths are those that concern me. In my own kingdom, I am aware of every level and sublevel in existence. I may not know all that goes on in each level, and I prefer it that way, but I will hear of any misdemeanours or crimes committed eventually. However, these lochs fill me with a foreboding – one that I have not experienced in several millennia.

I walk past the brightly coloured houses beside the pier in Tobermory and make my way to the farm where I left the horse. It's not far, and I notice, even from near the pier, that he is standing in the same place as when I left. In the distance, I watch as the groomsman leaves the stables carrying his saddle. I enter the man's mind and tell him to prepare the beautiful beast and I expect him to be ready in the next ten minutes, which is how long it will take for me to reach the farm.

As I enter the grounds, the horse begins to whinny in excited anticipation; I pat his nose and calm him, promising him the adventure he's been awaiting.

I mount him and settle comfortably on his back; he rises beautifully to the demands I make of him. It doesn't take long for me to have thrown off the troublesome adventure to the mainland as my trusty steed gallops in earnest towards Castle Moy.

I realise that, although I am not touching the ground, my horse is, and I am one with him as he all but flies through the air, with the merest of touches on the ground as he races.

I decide I prefer flying to being in a boat. Neither is on solid ground, but at least there is an element of control when in the air, and the earth is always in sight. In the water, I have no idea how far or how deep I may fall. There is also another possibility with respect to my dislike of water, and it is a fundamental one: water can douse the flames within my world, whereas air will only fan the flames that I enjoy.

With that thought in mind, I laugh out loud; I am ecstatic at this freedom I am enjoying. My coat flies out at the back of me; I feel the wind in my hair and my black beauty…

Oh, wait. I realise he is perspiring over much. He is being ridden too hard, and I have a fondness for this beast and don't want to destroy him because of my pleasure in this newfound release in my responsibilities. I pull him over to the side of the track, dismount and remove the saddle. The heat that comes from his body turns to steam, which rises in the cold air. I rub his body hard and allow him to rest, whilst I go behind a tree. What is it with this body that it leaks water every hour?

And that's when I see them. Two young lovers walking together. Oh, they don't have a clue I'm there. What they notice first is the horse with a blanket on his back, which to them is a bit suspect and makes them slightly wary, because there's no sign of the rider; they look around speculatively.

I watch them carefully. The girl has long, dark hair, which is tied back and falling down her back, underneath a bonnet that is tied under her chin. She's quite pretty, with large eyes, a small nose, a wide mouth and a ruddy complexion. She's wearing an apron and carrying a bundle under one arm, so I suspect she works in one of the castles. Her beau wears a wide hat; his hair is tied at the nape of his neck and is dark in colour, but not very long. His face is handsome enough, with dark eyes and a long nose. He smiles, and I can see he has a tooth missing; he looks to be a bit self-conscious of that because he covers his mouth with a hand. The girl laughs and knocks his hand away. He tucks his own bundle under his arm before reaching for her, grabbing her by the shoulders and pulling her close to kiss her.

I laugh quietly to myself and walk out from behind the tree, letting them know of my presence.

She espies me first, because he's too intent on kissing her, and, well, it's simply comical. Her hand flies to her mouth as it falls open, her eyes widen in fear and she pushes her lover away from her. He's not too happy at being rejected and recognises her terror slowly, then turns to look at whatever it is she is seeing. This time, when his mouth falls open, he's not bothered about the missing tooth that had him so self-conscious only moments earlier. His arms fall to his side, and he stands as though frozen.

"Good evening to you both," I say kindly. "Do you find yourself far from home?" I ask, then I wait. It doesn't take long...

Canny Scots that they are, the lovers hold fast to their belongings.

Here it comes...

Yes! If noises were wishes, I would have all of mine fulfilled simply by the screams emanating from these two before me. It's too funny. Not so close now, the lovers both turn and flee: the man runs through the forest and the girl runs north towards Tobermory.

I wasn't happy about not having a head, thanks to my angel brothers, but, as I watch the dirt on the track rise behind the girl as she makes her way as far from me as possible, I can see this is going to be a lot of fun.

"Now that was excellent, don't you think, Zamarkhan?" I say and pat his rump. "We would do well to go out each night and scare the locals, don't you think?"

The horse whinnies and I take it as a sign that he totally agrees with me, because he is the smartest beast I have ever met. I pat his nose and promise him extra hay; I might even clean out his stall – no, that's not going to happen – but I'll make sure the stable lad knows to treat him well, when we return to Moy.

"Are you ready to be ridden again, my beauty?" I query, and, wouldn't you know it, he actually nods.

I saddle up, jump on his back, pull one of the reins to turn him around and what do I see? I am incredulous to see where we have stopped; it surely is a sign that I should follow, if only I had more time, because right before my eyes stands Duart Castle, which is the castle belonging to MacLaine's brother. I do want to ride up and make the acquaintance of the laird, but I wonder if it is a bit premature.

I need MacLaine for the time being, and to antagonise him at this point in my venture might not be a wise decision.

It's not going anywhere. I make a mental note and, when the time is right, I'll return and cause some mischief, but first I have to put my plan into action.

Kicking the horse's flanks, I encourage him to move. There's no need to rush, so we ride at a decent pace, giving me time to consider what I should do next.

The damn plan should be what I do next. Instead of talking about it, I should be carrying it out, especially after having seen the little mistdreamers. The one who looked directly at me could see beyond my glamour. I know I have to move quickly on this, if only I knew what this should be! Where is my head? I don't mean the physical one; my brain is not functioning at all just now. Why can I not think straight? My legs feel weak, I'm nauseated and I'm tired. I'm Satan, for the love of Hell; I should be in peak condition, yet I'm as weak as a lamb.

Lamb? My stomach growls. That's it! I realise I'm hungry again. Not only does this body have to let water out every hour, it has to be restocked almost as regularly.

Moy can't be far, I think, so I give the horse another nudge, and we begin to move faster. Now that I know what the problem is, I can return to my musing.

Glencoe is definitely part of the plan; I have to go back to the exact date the Mistdreaming War took place, and that war isn't written into the annals of history. Thanks to Ambriel and Omniel, I have nothing stored in this brain. The war will not be listed in the angelic book – not that I have access to it at the moment. I have to speak to someone who was actually there at the time the war took place, but, yet again, I can curse my brothers for taking away my ability to travel through time.

Xaphan and Adramelechk are both involved; they could be the key to everything. I must remove them somehow, get access to those magical little boys and then kill them. Easy! If I had my powers.

I've been scuppered; the only decent thing my brothers have granted me is a minimal amount of my superb powers. I haven't really tried to examine what I can do or what may happen if I use them. I know that if I use any power, as I did earlier, I'll leave a trail of enchantment behind. The same will happen if I use sorcery; it would be able to be identified back to the source directly and open up my location to every supernatural being, and I want some semblance of privacy. If those boys can see me through all my glamour and protection, then I have to get hold of them; they will be the ones able to assist me in changing the past.

Without the need for any more delay, I nudge Zamarkhan into a gentle trot. He whinnies tosses his head, clearly unhappy at the lack of speed; he wants to let fly again, and I see no reason to give him more rein. Let us see how fast this glorious beast can go. After I tap a whip smartly to his side, he all but roars into the night air and off he goes, his hooves pummelling the ground. I do not believe I have ever felt this free, and I glory in the moment.

It is over all too quickly, as I soon see Moy ahead of me. Pulling on the reins, I slow Zamarkhan back to a trot, and we ride through the masses of ferns outside the castle. The sea air catches my throat, coming from the loch to my right, and I notice the volcanic sand on the beach is blacker that usual. The night sky is missing the stars, but the moon shines like a beacon, reflecting upon Lochbuie and giving light to the road ahead.

The castle stands on a rock at the head of the loch, and on a clear night you can see almost all the way Hector MacLaine's brother's castle, Duart. Beyond the castle, there is what we, in the other worlds, call a 'universal voice'; on Earth, nobody seems to know what it is, and they simply think it's a standing-stone circle. They have no idea that, on certain nights and for specific festivals such as Beltane, if you stand in the middle of the standing stones and turn in ten circles, citing the wishes of your dreams, the Fairy Queen has to appear and grant you the wish. What humans also don't know is that if the queen grants you this wish, she will ask a boon of you and, trust me, you don't want to be owing the Fairy Queen anything, because even I wouldn't want to owe her anything.

I ride close to the castle, and I see Hector waiting for me at the castle door. When I jump down from the horse, a stable boy takes Zamarkhan's reins from my hands – he doesn't even look up at me – and walks towards the stables.

I shout to him, "Make sure he gets extra hay and brush him down hard."

There is no response, only a nod of his head as he pulls the horse towards the stables.

*

Zamarkhan trots happily behind the boy, eager to be free of the saddle on his back. He's enjoyed the ride, but his master has been a cruel one, so he's galloped faster than normal, just to be rid of him. When the lad removes the tack, he swears he can hear the horse sigh in relief, and when the bag of oats is placed before the animal, Zamarkhan whinnies in joy. He is home and will avoid the Devil at any cost.

*

"Ye took yer time, did ye no'?" is my warm greeting from the laird. I shake his hand and pat him on the back, moving into the castle.

"I need to get warmed; it's a long ride to Tobermory, and an even longer trip to Mingary, but it was worth it," I explain.

Hector frowns at me. "Did ye carry oot all the devilment ye wanted? Wis there chaos left that ah'll hae tae clear up when ye decide tae leave us?"

I'm surprised by the venom in his voice, and I arch one eyebrow. "Are you talking to me, Hector, or has your body been replaced by someone else?"

Hector turns his back on me and stomps into the great room; he looks over his shoulder and barks, "Get ye tae sit doun here by the fire." He points at the large wing-backed chair, with a footstool in front of it, and irritated, ushers me to sit before continuing, "It'll warm ye soon, then ye can get on yer way tae wherever it is ye want tae go, an' leave me an' mine tae oor own devices. But…" He waits until I have sat and warmed my hands at the flames that are flaring angrily up into the chimney. "I warn ye no' tae be duplicit in yer promises. Even ah, a mere mortal, can arrange for yer demise."

Now that is a surprise; how would this be possible? Could it be that this laird is more cunning than I first thought or is he in league with my angel brothers?

The room is dark, and a serving wench comes in, carrying a tray with two beakers and a jug, which she lays upon a small table beside the chair opposite mine. Her eyes are glazed over, and I know she's in a trance; she's been enchanted so as to not fear my headless body.

"Aye, ah can see whit yer thinkin', an' the answer is no. Ah'll hae nothin' tae dae wi' angels," he says as he hands me a tumbler of whisky before continuing with his rant. "Tae be 'onest, ah'd hae nothin' tae dae wi' ye, had ye no' turned up on ma doorstep an' promised me ye'd put things right wi' me an' ma brother. So ah'll be holdin' ye tae yer promise, or else."

That is it! I've had enough. First of all, I'm sore from all the riding I've done, despite the amazing work of Zamarkhan; this mortal body has places in it that ache whenever I move, and I have mentally patted myself on the back on several occasions for not losing my temper. However, I'm sore, I'm wet, I'm cold and I'm miserable; I have no powers, I'm nowhere near the place I'd hoped to be, my brothers have bespelled me, I'm no longer king of my own castle, and here is a puny mortal telling me what to do, else he'll sort me out.

I throw the tumbler into the fire, and it smashes against the kerb; the flames fly higher, and the tapestry nearby gets singed, but doesn't catch fire.

To give the laird his due, he stands his ground in the presence of one as great as me and, in my fury, I have to admit to him being a very formidable sight. With his legs apart, and him holding onto his whisky, the only noticeable thing that may indicate he is alarmed is that his eyes widen for a second. His arms and legs do not tremble; he even sips his whisky, then raises one eyebrow in question, as though I'm a spoilt child having a tantrum.

I want to send him to the fires of Hell and get one of my demons to show him exactly how powerful I am, and I watch him smirk at me! Yes, smirk!

I grab him by the tartan waistcoat he wears and slam him into the wall, three feet from the ground. Where was this strength when I needed it earlier? Now I note his fear, which brings pleasure. My ears are ringing; I'm so angry that my nails turn to talons and lengthen, and I begin to tear at his neck. He has gone still in my arms and stares at me with hard, black eyes, and I know I have gone too far.

I drop him to the floor and he stands immediately and dusts himself down. "Did ye like that, aye?" he asks and his face turns a bright red.

I hadn't known I'd stopped the flow of his blood.

"Ye need tae move on, Nick; 'tis time ye left ma castle," he continues.

"You're kicking me out?" I cannot believe the cheek of the man.

"I'm tellin' ye, it's time tae go aboot yer business. Yer no' supposed tae be on this Earth; ye ken ye hae yer ane home, an' it's no' here. Ye're only goin' tae mak problems here, an' they're ones we humans will hae tae sort oot, an' that's no' really what ye came here for, is it?"

Why is this man making so much sense? "I do have a problem, you know that, but I need some more time to work out the particulars."

"When ye're finished, ye can return; Ah'll no' turn ye away, but remember yer promise; ye'll assist me wi' ma brother Lachlan. It's a problem that must be put tae bed, an', wi' yer help, ah'll finally see the back o' him an' tak control o' his castle once an' for all."

"Haven't you done that already?" I ask.

"Aye, we battled, an' I won so it became ma castle, then he raised his ane army an' took control o' Moy; that was unacceptable. Oor next battle must be the last, an' he has tae realise ah'm the yin with the power, not him," he fumed.

I've had enough of him. "I need some air." I walk away, leaving him to smoulder, lost in his own thoughts of battle and power.

I step out of the castle into the cold air and look up to the velvety, dark-blue sky; the clouds have cleared, and the stars are now shining, along with the bright moon, yet the land is shrouded in mist. The loch cannot be seen, but I can hear the waves ebbing and flowing in the gentle breeze, then lapping against the land.

I like it here. Oh, it doesn't have the wealth of power I have in my own kingdom, but there is peace, which is something I haven't experienced for a very long time. I lose myself in the tranquillity, my restlessness is banished and I am only disturbed by the sound of the ferns rustling. I'm actually smiling as I look upon the mass of them, until I see movement amongst them. I walk towards the movement, and know what and who has been watching me.

"Come out, mistdreamer," I order.

The young boy removes himself from his hiding place and comes towards me. I'm impressed with his bravery, as not many would face me down. Yet, here I am, looking down into the swirling, blue-and-green eyes of a magical human.

I realise now that this is no ordinary mistdreamer – this is one of the ancients – and so I must tread carefully when dealing with such a being. This is yet another item that has been omitted by Flauros. I stroke my chin and regard him methodically. He stands straight in front of me, with a wooden sword in his hand, wearing a kilt and shirt with a plaid across his chest. He's a warrior.

I have to laugh. "You come near me? You know what I can do to you, don't you, mistdreamer?"

He remains standing and growls – yes, growls – at me. "O' course ah ken who ye are. Ye're the Deil."

Now this is interesting; he can see past the headless horseman. "And who might you be?"

"Ye're talkin' tae Christopher Graeme Park MacLain of Acharacle," he replies proudly.

I hunker down to his size and look directly into his eyes. "Mighty big name for someone so small in stature."

"Ah'll grow," he answers simply.

I'm taken aback by his audacity and laugh out loud. "That is the truth for sure, and yet you dare to come here to see me? For what reason? Do you intend to kill me?" I stop grinning when I note the seriousness that crosses his face. "What is it, mistdreamer? What secrets do you have that I may not have knowledge of?"

Christopher takes a deep intake of breath, as though bored with my company already. "Ah ken ye're the Devil, Nick Mahoun; ah can see yer heid an' ah ken ye've loast yer powers."

Nine

I wait with bated breath to hear more from this little horror.

"Ah ken all aboot ye an' how ye cannae get back tae yer hame," he says quite officiously.

"Hmm," I mutter and put my hands on my hips. "I ken… I know how to get back to my own home, thank you very much," I impress on him.

It's a sight I cannot believe, but this little boy actually giggles at me!

"Yer daft. Ye need us mistdreamers tae aid ye, 'cause you're loast," he continues.

"I am not," I insist.

"Aye, ye are," he bounces back. "Ye're no' supposed tae be on Mull; it's miles from where ye're supposed tae be. Ye got all footered around when ye came into oor world."

I wait and I sigh; I want to kill him. I cross my arms over my chest. "How did you get here?" I ask.

Christopher smiles, then covers his lips, eyeing me slyly to see my reaction, and I refuse to bite but wait for what it is he will tell me.

"That wud be the mermaids," he says.

I feel as though someone has punched this mortal body; the pain that shoots through me hearing those fearful words. Mermaids! It can't be true. I rid this world of them centuries ago, and none survived; I made sure of that.

"Ye dinnae need tae pretend yer no' scared; ah ken ye are. Mermaids can bind ye forever, can they no'?" He chortles. He turns his back to me, and I see him rubbing his chin, just as I had done moments ago. "Is it mebbe a wee possibility that ah ken o' a place whereby ye can be bound?"

"No," I shout, "it is not, and I've had enough of this. Get to the point, mistdreamer, or ride away on whatever it is that brought you to this place; you're not welcome here."

"Ye ken ah'm tellin' the truth o' it; ah can see it in yer fearful eyes. Ye ken ye missed some o' them now, dae ye no'?" he says coldly.

I'm furious; I grab handfuls of cloth on my jacket and squeeze hoping for the anger to abate, but the little monster hasn't finished with me yet.

"An' ye ken that if ye step out o' order when ye're here, ah'll ken… know, what ye're up tae an' ah promise ye, Nick Mahoun, that ah'll hae ye wrapped up like a baby in a blanket an' ah'll hide ye so far from anyone or anything's sight, that ye'll be beggin' tae be let go."

I can't stand listening to him anymore. His words are hitting me like darts, and his melodic voice hurts my ears; it's as though he's enchanting me and whispering a spell over me. I explode, my nails lengthen, my eyes seep black, and I can feel my teeth growing longer. I arch my back and ready myself to pounce on him, but I don't get the chance. Before I move, Christopher raises his hand, his palm facing me, with disdain in his eyes. "That's nae goin' tae happen, beast," he snarls.

I'm suspended in the air, I feel invisible ties around my body, and I can't move a muscle. My hair is flying all round my face, making it difficult for me to look down and see the mistdreamer, who remains holding his hand steadfastly in the air facing me. And then, to my horror, he twirls his forefinger, and I begin to spin until my stomach starts to churn. My eyes fly open in horror when next he flicks his finger. I have no idea what's going to happen.

I'm thrust through the air and have no control of my destiny; I look back to the mistdreamer, who is pointing. I can't turn my head to see where is he pointing and where I'm going subsequently, but then I feel the hard granite pound into my back as I strike the castle wall. My body crumbles, I fall to the ground, and the pain causes me to pass out.

When my eyes flutter open eventually, the mistdreamer is standing over me, his face full of anger and contempt.

"Dinnae try that again an' dinnae think, for one moment, ye frighten me, beast," he says stroppily, his finger pointing at me.

I cower, waiting to find out what it is he intends to do to me.

Instead, he puts his hand into his pocket. "Ah'm warnin' ye, it's best no' tae mak a fool o' me, Nick; ah'll no' stand it. If ye try any o' yer nonsense, it'll be the mermaids who'll deal wi' ye."

He bends down and puts his nose to mine. I see depths in his eyes that are so fathomless that I hold my breath. They go beyond the realms of mine, and I have to admit to being slightly uneasy. I recall the terror I saw when I did the same to Flauros and have an instant regret at my action. I am quite shocked when a thought flashes through my mind about making amends with my duke, but it is a fleeting notion and one that comes only as a consequence of being ensnared by a small boy, and I'm deeply embarrassed – but only for a moment.

Now I'm just angry.

He pulls away from me, announcing, "Ah'll help ye once. Whit is it ye want?"

Sitting up, I give a definite answer: "I want to right the wrongs done to my demons."

Turning from me, he shouts over his shoulder, "That's no' goin' tae happen."

He's not far from me; I could pounce on him and ready myself to make my move, but my back is in agony, and all I do is fall on my face. I pull myself from the ground and straighten my clothes; I am very wary of this little person. "Tell me how you can help me, mistdreamer?" I ask.

I know he's studying me, as his eyes are searching my body and probing my mind.

When I've had enough of his insolence and move towards him, he tells me, "Ah will let ye ken whit it is ye can an' cannae dae whilst yer stuck here on Earth."

I am controlling my temper admirably; however, his impudence is causing all manner of chemical reactions in my brain, and I can feel my anger beginning to erupt once more. In my defence, it really isn't my fault! I take a glance at the castle wall, and the memory of slamming into it is enough to make me cool down. I do think, though, that it is criminal that I am dependent upon a five-year-old – no matter how ancient his soul is – to guide me, the master of Hell, whilst I stay on Earth! But, as they say here on Earth, "Needs must. When the devil drives."

I wait for a few moments, believing I am now in control of the situation, but, in truth, knowing I am like a boat without a rudder, floundering in an ocean of uncertainty.

"Fine," I answer finally. "Tell me, little mistdreamer, how is it you intend to aid me on my mission?"

"Ah'll no' be assistin' ye on any mission," he insists; he scratches his head and his fine, blond hair tangles underneath his fingers. "Ah'm only goin' tae tell ye the rules that ye have tae follow and some things ye might no' ken."

He speaks like an old man, I think to myself. I nod, waiting to hear what else he has to offer.

"For a start," he begins, "sit doun; ye're giein' me a crick in ma neck."

I sit beside him immediately, and he touches my nose, as though he is simply a child playing with a friend or family member. It's a sensation that has me discombobulated and makes me very uncomfortable because it is a sweet, innocent gesture. I shake myself out of these impure thoughts – those thoughts I had before the angels rid me of my warmth when they took away my heart.

"Ye dinnae need tae ride a horse or go in a boat; ye can blink yersel' anywhere an' tae any time in Scotland."

"Any time?" I query.

"Aye, ye're still able tae dae that. Ye can blink yersel' all the way back tae the war, if that's yer intended time an' place."

I smile as he sits beside me and crosses his legs, pulling his kilt between them for dignity's sake, and he rubs his neck, his eyes growing heavy with tiredness.

Again, that damn feeling of compassion strays into my heart. He is a beautiful child. I have to remember how dangerous he is and purge myself of any tender feelings I may have towards him, but it is difficult, and these human emotions are beginning to get the better of me.

I reach out and stroke his hair. In horror, I pull my hand back quickly and ask gruffly, "Is that it? I just blink. That's all you have for me?"

"Aye, there's more," he says solemnly, "Ye can blink yersel' back tae that war; ye ken, the war that killed ma parents?"

I wonder where this conversation is heading and I can see the little lad is annoyed, but holding his emotions in check. Maybe this would be a way to poke the sleeping dog and get a rise out of him? I look at the castle wall again; perhaps not.

"Your parents were involved in a war, they were killed, and I'm sorry for you that it happened, but they chose to be part of the battle; they were casualties of war, as were my dukes, princes and demons," I explain.

Christopher appears to mull over what I've said. "Aye, but youse started it," he replies bitterly, pointing his finger at me.

Sparks fly in every direction, and I launch myself to the ground just as one of the flashes lands beside me, burning the ferns and smouldering hotly.

"Okay, okay." I put my hand up in surrender. "We're veering off the point of this discussion. Surely we can deal with this problem later?" I ask, and sit back into position slowly, opposite the child who now is as composed as a stone Buddha.

"What was the last thing you told me…" I quickly add, before he has the opportunity to reply, "about going back in time, not about your parents?"

Christopher chuckles and, using his hand, gently strokes the earth nearby. The motion of his hand is mesmerising and I can't take my eyes from it.

"Aye," he giggles.

I am brought back to reality immediately; that voice, soft and soothing, is grating on my nerves, and I know he is about to give me a mental thump.

He goes on, "Ye can go forwards an' backwards in time. Ye can mingle an' talk wi' those there, an' ye might even learn a thing or two," he says pointedly, "but here's the rub o' it…"

I wait for the sucker punch.

He smiles and looks deep into my eyes. "Ye'll no' be able tae change anythin' in the past. If ye try, there'll be consequences."

I think for a moment; the punch hasn't been as bad as I'd expected. "Such as?" I ask.

Christopher shakes his head from side to side – with enthusiasm, just as any five-year-old does – and grins beguilingly at me. "Just try it," he whispers menacingly, "and ye'll find oot."

Boom! Right there in my solar plexus, that's where it hits me again. This little runt is toying with me; he is the one with the power, he is controlling me, and I won't have it. Not ever! The sooner I leave his company, the sooner I can get the job done and return to my own kingdom.

"How is it that I can get to these places? You know, the ones I can't change anything in but can only learn from," I sneer.

"Och, that's simple," he says as he stands and brushes his kilt free of earth. "All ye hae tae dae is think yersel' there. Imagine the place in yer mind an' be specific aboot the time ye want tae reach, but remember, O dark one…" He points that finger at me again, and I shrink away from him. "Remember," he continues "that should ye attempt tae travel further than the bonds o' space, or interfere wi' time, then ye'll ken what'll happen."

I ignore this repeated warning. "I just need to imagine myself in a place and the time I want to be there, and that's it?" I search the boy's face for some truth in this statement. "Then tell me, boy, how is it that, when first I arrived, I thought of places but was unable to get there?" I poke his chest, then poke him again. "Well," I yell, "give me the answer to that one."

"Ye ken," the little runt says as he grabs my finger and somehow manages to bend it back 180° – as he answers I can barely hear him over my screaming – "for a supernatural king an' master o' his own kingdom, ye really are kind o' stupid, aren't ye?"

He screws his face up and shakes his head in disbelief, then releases my finger, which I grab hold of, with my throbbing finger causing pain like I cannot believe. I just look at it as it swells up and turns purple, then turn to him incredulous that he has inflicted such grief upon myself.

"How could you do that to me?" I am in shock "Get rid of the pain, mistdreamer!"

"Whit a wuss ye are," he says, then grabs my finger, which causes me to scream even louder until, amazingly, warmth floods into me, the pain is gone and my finger has righted itself into the correct position.

I stare at him – half in wonder, half in fear – and know it's time for me to leave.

"Yer powers are granted through me an' ma brother, an' can be taken away by us, so behave yersel' on ye travels. We'll always ken where ye are, an' if ye get up tae mischief, we'll sort ye oot," he confirms.

I have no doubt of that and merely nod my head in acceptance. "Think, imagine, blink; I think even I, a stupid supernatural king, can manage that."

"Then what're ye waitin' for? It's time tae go, Nick Mahoun, but ah ken we'll be seeing ye again; hopefully, later rather than sooner."

I am in total agreement with him and close my eyes, envisaging my destination and timeframe, and, wouldn't you know, the little mistdreamer was right.

Ten

I've never been fond of Glencoe. I don't mean its natural beauty; it is one of the most beautiful sights on Earth, even I can appreciate that. The massive range of mountains rises up like overgrown guards standing in protection of the lush, expansive, green land, which is scattered with rocks that look like rubble from a distance, but, as you near them, you realise they're boulders. The erratics – massive boulders left behind from the ice-age – are spread sporadically across the vast ground, making it more obvious they are out of place, standing alone and completely different from the mass of rocks on the ground. The bountiful lochs shimmer as though fairies are dancing upon the waves and reflect the land all around, like a giant mirror, then, suddenly, the image breaks into a million pieces as the wind catches the waves.

It is a bleak place, which whispers the history of the dead in its captivating beauty; it is a place where a soul can mend in the reverent silence beneath the watchful eyes of the magnificent sentinels that cast their shadows upon the ground.

It is also the Veil: the door to other worlds, watched over by a body of angels who prevent – as far as possible – humans crossing into these worlds. Mistakes happen; humans always stretch themselves, and some believe the ultimate exercise is to climb a mountain and, unfortunately for some, they fall. In that fall, they will find themselves taken into another world, and those angels guarding the Veil are unable to prevent the fallen passing through the secret passage. The humans never make their way into my world. Those pesky angels ensure that my world is closed to any human who traverses accidentally through the Veil.

Another reason I dislike Glencoe is that it is also the place where the Mistdreaming War took place and where my demons were destroyed. My kings were sent to another universe, which is one that I cannot get access to because of the guardians of the Veil.

I'm fairly sure they know I'm in their territory, as the weather has taken a downturn and, instead of the sunshine I had become accustomed to on Mull, I am soaking wet with the downpour of heavy rain. I'm fairly certain it's meant to send me in the wrong direction, and I will admit I feel a little lost, but I'm determined. I will find the problem here somewhere.

I look around the desolate beauty and imagine the war that destroyed my demons.

Flauros had attempted to relate to me the events that occurred, but he'd missed out a lot. It was difficult to perceive that my strong beasts could be defeated by the likes of angels and mistdreamers. Of course, they had the help of the fae and their brothers, the dragons. Still, my demons are outstanding in hand-to-hand combat, and there's no chance they would have fallen easily.

A voice in my head laughs; it sounds almost like the mistdreamer Christopher, but somehow I know it must be his twin, Paul. They even named him after Xaphan, he who betrayed me.

"You betrayed yourself," the soft voice whispers, "Look. Look ahead and see what really happened."

Still pictures appear before me, which are clips of the battle, and I study them carefully. I cannot understand where and how my army was beaten.

"Look closer," the voice whispers.

Suddenly, the battle is in front of me, like watching a movie but being part of the action.

There is Lucias, his contemptuous face gloating as he recognises three witches. He has intended to kill one and feed off the others. Lying on the ground is his mother's head; in his anger, he has decapitated her.

He believes the witches will save him. I can see he has already made an exit plan for if that isn't the case. He isn't concentrating, just wallowing in his own future and believing his plans are brilliant, so he doesn't hear the flapping of gigantic wings.

I look up as the sky darkens and see an army of dragons, all intent on battle.

I watch as they swoop down towards my demons; it's a precise strategy and enforced meticulously.

I can hear the sound of bones snapping and limbs being ripped off. After a short while, the leading dragon pulls upwards, away from dragons lost in the kill and leaves the chaos of demon destruction being carried out on the ground; he rejoins the group of dragons that had followed.

They ready themselves for another attack at the far end of the glen, realigning into an arrow formation, then speed towards my army. My demons wait for the clash and charge towards them, but the dragons hover in anticipation. I can hear Lucias screaming at the demons to withdraw, but he's too late; the dragons attack with ferocity, with their steel wings drowning out his orders.

I want to cover my eyes; I cannot bear to see what may happen next, but I can hear the dragon taking in deep breaths and it's fairly clear what they intend to do. The leader of one troupe begins to blow softly until a spark lights her exhalation. The rest of the group follow likewise, exhaling then waiting for the mixture of oxygen and carbon monoxide to light. When all the dragons' breaths are alight, they flap their wings, aim at my demons and blow the fire at them. A wave of dragon fire sets my demons on fire; some scatter, leaving them as easy prey for those battling fae and mistdreamers on the ground, and for dragons hovering in the air.

The cunning fae are disappearing then reappearing behind the demons, turning my people into demonic spinning tops.

I watch in horror as waves of fire light dried grass and stray pieces of wood, slithering like ferocious fiery snakes, searching for prey. When it touches my demons, they disappear into a cloud of ash, which then floats to the earth like grey snowflakes. Other flames wind their way towards other demons, who turn and run, making sure the flames can't reach them. But it's too far for them to help the remaining demons who are still fighting on the field. They begin to march back to help, and I gasp when I see angels diving at them, with their wings lying backwards, giving them the ability to fly faster.

Meanwhile, the fae are still using their magic, disappearing then appearing again, stabbing to the rear and to the sides until the demons fall.

I want to grab Lucias and rip him apart when he begins to cast a spell. He is blowing his breath into the air and flicking his finger into his poisonous breath. With each flick, he creates a deathly flying creature, and I watch as the dragons retreat, waiting for the command from my Prince of Hell, Seere – and here's where I begin to feel nauseous, because I watch as he aids the dragon in defeating his own brother demons. He orders the dragon to prepare for attack then belches out fire, destroying Lucias's magical creatures.

At this point, I'm not sure who I hate the most, Seere or Lucias.

My demons are taking a hammering, and I shout at them to retreat, but, of course, they can't hear me. I hear the sound of a thousand voices and the marching of another army, and can't believe my eyes as another army of fae enters the glen.

My own angel brothers appear to assist in the battles. This is surely the most uneven battle ever; a bit like an army of hunters using high-powered rifles to shoot grazing goats, with my demons being the goats!

The mistdreamer Mairi is there; I watch her bid farewell to two people before walking with the fae and angels into the foray.

Good grief! Is that Michael also? I notice him, the archangel warrior, making his entrance with a brilliant, white light. Damn it, my demons are now trapped between the fae, an army of angels and hovering dragons, and Michael stands front and centre, leading the charge.

What the hell? Lucias is leaving his men and going after the mistdreamer; he's even covered himself with an invisibility glamour, the little sneak. Why is he not battling beside them? Because he's a damn coward, that's why. I point at Flauros, who's now made his appearance. He's not intent on anything other than Lucias. I'd given orders to kill him and, to my pleasure, I can see he's trying to carry out my demands.

The sounds of screaming rend the cold air; they're the sounds coming from my demons.

My king Dantalian is fighting, but he loses his stance when the angel Raphael grabs his hair and zooms into the air. Dantalian twists around and turns into a leopard. Raphael lets him fall to the earth. As he lands, Dantalian loses his footing and slides into the erratics before, eventually, crashing into a tree. Stunned, he shakes his head and re-forms into a human.

What on earth? The erratics are changing shape. Huge masses of stone are turning into Highlanders.

I watch as Dantalian's head is smashed in with a hammer.

The battle is surely over when I notice the archangels turning into a cloud of mist, then rising above the demons. Tiny droplets of their blood drip onto the demons and they sizzle upon contact. Re-forming upon the Earth, the archangels take their magnificent swords and run through the screaming, twisting demons, who turn into balls of fire. When a supernatural wind blows through the glen, it picks up their ash remains and carries it away from Glencoe, disposing of it far from the dead already slain and lying in the ground.

My king Amdusias is trapped, but looks resigned; I watch as another of my dukes, this time Vual, is murdered by a woman whilst he is in chains awaiting being sent back to Hell. Oh the unfairness of it all! This is not following any rule-book conventions for battle, and, because it's angels and fae, they'll be depicted as the 'good' side, whilst my demons will be shown to be on the wrong side.

It's a sorry state of affairs altogether, and I take no comfort when I witness the deaths of the mistdreamer boys' parents, Appoloin and Mairi; it is a senseless end.

It was all senseless and all because of that little runt Lucias.

Thinking the movie is over, I turn away from the images only to return swiftly to viewing when I catch a glimpse of something in the corner of the screen.

It's me! I was at this battle? Why is it that I have no memory of this?

Michael is standing talking with me, and then I'm no longer in the picture.

Where did I go? What happened after that? Why is it I have no memory of this?

The images disappear, and I'm back on my own, leaning against a boulder in Glencoe. I allow myself time to think about everything I've just seen. My demons didn't stand a chance; Lucias led them into a massacre, and I'm lucky any of them returned home alive. My plan now must change; no longer am I interested in changing the events that occurred, instead I want to find Lucias and destroy him.

The ground is wet beneath my feet, but I must rest for a moment, and take stock of the situation and the changes that must be made. As I lean against the giant erratic to catch my breath, my legs are weak, so I sit on the ground and lay my head on the stone. I close my eyes for a moment, trying to decipher everything that has been shown to me.

I feel a slight rumble beneath me and open my eyes, looking in all directions to discover what the cause is of the noise.

The earth begins to move suddenly, and I jump up, steadying myself by holding onto the erratic. The ground moves beneath my feet, shaking and rocking, then the earth is folded turbulently away from me. Rocks begin to tumble and race down the slopes, and the ground rolls like frothing waves.

The erratic shudders under my touch, and I jump back in time to watch the stone dissolve into a waterfall of stars that fall into the earth. In its place, stands a Highlander in full battle dress, with his sword at his side, his targe held in front of his chest and his bonnet hanging over to one side, lying above his ear. He's not what I'd call a handsome man, certainly not as handsome as I; he's as wide as he is tall, with a large barrel chest, and powerful arms and shoulders. His beard is grey and touches his chest, and his piercing blue eyes don't miss mine as he stares angrily at me.

"And who might you be?" I ask as nonchalantly as my voice will allow.

If it's possible, he stands even straighter. "I am the MacIain, the twelfth chief of Glencoe, and I think you already know who I am, but are merely delaying until you can get your head around what it is you see."

"I've seen a lot worse," I answer sarcastically.

"I've no doubt you have, and are probably the cause of most of the bad you've seen."

I shake my head in denial, then change my mind. "You're probably right there," I agree.

"Why have you come onto our lands again? You take your life into your own hands when you stand here, especially with the guardians protecting us."

"They didn't do much good for you not so long ago, did they?"

"Perfidy," he yells, "treachery, that even the guardians were unaware of, an' you were the ring leader. Ye deserve all that's comin' tae ye!" His accent has changed into the brogue of Scotland.

"I had nothing at all to do with the Campbell's fight with you. I do not have complete control over my dukes and kings, despite what you believe. I am not my Father; I give my people free rein. If it comes to my ears that I have been deceived, then I will intervene."

"So why are ye here?" he asks me.

"Because I was deceived during the Mistdreaming War and I want to make amends to correct the situation."

"There was nae deception caused tae ye in that war; it was a fair battle, won by the better side."

"The better side had more assistance, and it was an unequal battle."

"Ye'd better hold yer tongue, Nick; else ah'll cast ye back tae Hell's pit where ye belong."

Hmph, I'd like to see him try, I think to myself.

"Ye cannae correct whit has happened, so why even try? Are ye no' awfy fed up wi' all this anger an' fightin'?"

"Well, come to think of it," I say, "I am very tired; I could do with a break. It's exhausting always having to clean up messes made by lesser demons, and not knowing until the last minute what my kings have done and how they… regularly… fail. Then there's the punishment…"

"Aye, well, let's no' go doun that road an' stay on this yin, aye?"

As with most Highlanders – well, most Scots – he's direct and to the point; there's no need to add fancy language and no need to go around in circles hoping you will understand what they mean eventually. I like this man.

"What is it you want to know?" I ask him.

"What dae ye want tae dae? Ye ken ye cannae change time or events, so why dinnae ye tak a holiday? Go sightseeing an' dae whit tourists in the future dae: stay in a comfy hotel, be pampered, walk around the touns o' Scotland or wherever it is ye want tae be, an' just enjoy yersel.'"

I laugh out loud, holding my stomach as it rumbles, again. "You think that I, the lord of decadence and depravity, need to go on a holiday?"

He rubs his beard, contemplatively. "Aye, sometimes even youse need a break from depravity. Ye need tae be amongst people an' no' demons, just tae feel whit it is we're like. Ye've lost yer way an' made a contented kingdom, ye thought, but, surely, even youse need a break from it at times? Elsewise, why are ye here?"

"I'm here because I wanted to right the Mistdreaming War, but have found I am blocked at every turn by mistdreamers or angels, and I cannot carry out the mission I intended."

"Aye, it's a sair fecht when ye cannae dae whit ye hoped for, so why no' change whit ye intended noo that ye've discovered it's impossible?"

Why is this Scotsman making sense? My head feels as though it's spinning, and his words hit me like stings from a wasp. They're bearable but uncomfortable.

"A holiday, you say?" I ask. The idea is beginning to take root.

"A holiday," he reiterates, "A time away from work where ye can forget aboot work, enjoy the weather, laugh wi' people, see the sites an' enjoy the beauty. Dae ye think yer capable o' enjoying beauty or are ye so evil that ye can nae longer see the truth?"

"I am the Devil, the king of Hell," I say simply, "I am evil."

He hums and haws. "Then mayhap, a holiday is no' tae yer likin'?" he asks with a concerned voice.

I am taken aback by his concern; this isn't supposed to happen to me. I am met with fear and anger, not concern. I listen to him when he continues.

"Even evil taks a holiday. Ye shud try it; ye might even hae the type o' fun the rest o' the world experiences. Who kens, ye might decide tae stay." Then he takes a deep breath before discounting that idea. "But ah wud suggest that doesn't happen; we don't want tae see Hell being loosed on the world because ye're on holiday."

"So, you're condemning me to eternity in Hell with no reprieve?" I laugh.

"Ye did that yersel' when ye got jealous o' us mere mortals, without gieing us a chance tae redeem oorsels in yer eyes."

I don't want to hear this. I don't want to hear the truth; it hurts. I want to escape this place, to go anywhere, but avoid everything. He's right, this chieftain; it's time for the Devil to take a holiday. "I thank you for the advice. It's made me think, and you're right; I'm going somewhere that I can get lost as a tourist. I'm going on vacation."

The chieftain is startled, but smiles when he watches me close my eyes and think of the place I wanted to be.

"Just blink," said the mistdreamer who had entered my thoughts, "And ye'll be there."

And so I did.

Eleven

As much as I dislike Glencoe, I have to admit to loving Edinburgh.

Oh, it has nothing to do with its twelfth-century castle, though Edinburgh claims it to be ninth century – hmm, I have my doubts there, perhaps one of the foundations was that century – anyway, I digress. It isn't even the millions-of-years-old dead volcano, though I would love to restore that volcano and make it boil again; wouldn't it be fun watching all the people run around during the Edinburgh International Festival, trying to escape lava? Maybe not! It also has nothing to do with the Royal Mile, the Palace of Holyrood or the filming of *Outlander*, because – let's be honest – it's not really always filmed in Edinburgh. Neither is it the filming of *Rebus, North and South, Taggart* or so many others that I can't be bothered naming.

It has everything to do with the possibility of discovering witches. They will be my salvation, as it is they who will return me to my kingdom of Hell.

I walk along the George IV Bridge; it's teeming with people. I have arrived on 8th August, smack bang in the middle of the Edinburgh Festival.

It is good to note that I am no longer in the sixteenth century, as I've been carried by my 'blink' to the twenty-first century. This is a century I am more comfortable in: there's less truth and more debauchery! There's easy access to manipulation, and, with a population open to more beliefs than even I knew existed, I'm bound to find a church that worships the dark arts. How easy it will be to work my way into that congregation and persuade them to do as I ask.

I am surrounded by every nation in the world, and have yet to hear an Edinburgh accent; it would appear when the world descends upon Edinburgh, Edinburgh leaves!

I bump into a few people:

"Excusa."

"συγνώμη"

"Scusa."

"借口"

"言い訳"

"Izvinite."

"Izgovor."

"Excusez-moi!"

"Move, ya daft bam!"

And that's the comment that got my attention. I wanted the voice to belong to a woman, but instead it's a man – and a very tall man at that – wearing a kilt. I think it's a kilt, as it has pleats and a pin, but it's not tartan.

This pleases me; the clans are far too possessive of their tartans. I have whispered into many a mortal ear, persuading them to get rid of the kilt and the tartan! I'm glad I have been listened to and must search to find the person who put my whispers into action, because that would be an easy mind to bend.

Has tartan changed that much in the twenty-first century that they no longer need to wear clan tartans or have they run out of the threads required to make the tartan? I search around me, and the answer to both of these definitely is no, because I can see the tartan of the clans is being worn by others.

But where should I start?

I jostle another few people. Some are apologetic like those earlier, and a few have accents that sound as though they are from the Americas; their speech is strange, as they omit nouns for a start: "What's with?" and "Come with." Please explain!

I follow the tall man onto the cobbled Royal Mile, look to my left, and there's Edinburgh Castle, looming over the city, but I can't see where the tall man is. I look right and I can see St Giles Church and the Tron Church in the distance, with its distinctive steeple that reminds me of a witch's hat, yet there is no sign of the tall man.

Looking ahead, I spy the Bank of Scotland, which sits at the top of the Mound and is the once-upon-a-time head office of that banking group. It is a Georgian-style villa with a unique, green domed roof.

I see the man again; there he is, ahead of me in the distance. I watch him walk down the Mound and follow him. I expect him to walk towards Princes Street, which is the main street in Edinburgh; instead, he turns left and walks up Mound Place, a continuous road that changes into Ramsay Lane, which then takes me to – Royal Mile.

What on earth?

I keep following him, hiding in doorways, not that it's necessary because the mere volume of people will keep me hidden from anyone's view; however, it's better to be safe than sorry. I notice he's turned right and is now walking towards the castle's esplanade; it's almost as if he's aware that he might be being followed and is taking measures to ensure he isn't seen. He blends in with the crowd, as do I; however, I've been following him for twenty minutes and he stands out in the crowd. He looks furtively over his shoulder, and I stand with a group of tourists, pretending to be part of the walking group. At the same time, I notice him continue walking towards the castle.

There's something about him that is vaguely familiar.

I watch as he ducks down – he's too tall for the ancient doorframe – and enters a restaurant. I amble along with the group, half-listening to the tour operator as she explains how witches used to be thrown off the ledge of the castle esplanade into the Nor Loch, which is the moat that once surrounded Edinburgh Castle. I see him sitting at a table. He's scrutinising the room; is he expecting someone? I turn my back to him, in case he catches a glimpse of me studying him, and feign interest in the tour guide. When I look back, he's gone! Damnation!

I search all around, in the hope I will find he left the restaurant, but there is no sign of him. Instead, I decide to enter and check for myself, and perhaps get a better chance to have a good look at him and see if I recognise him.

I'm greeted by the hostess, and she is pleased by what she sees. Why wouldn't she be? I'm a handsome man and do admit to being pleasantly surprised at meeting such a beauty so quickly into my visit. I had thought it would take a few days before I found some interest, but here it is – staring at me in the face, checking out my body and smiling at what she obviously wants.

"May I help you, sir?" she asks.

"You definitely may," I answer, with a small smile on my face as I try to keep my voice steady and non-lecherous.

She's clearly taken aback, and I'm surprised by her reaction; have I read her previous actions incorrectly?

She lays a hand on my arm and smiles up into my eyes, lowering her eyelids coyly. Her black eyelashes fan across her cheekbones; she is a beauty, but I don't want to rush this and get it wrong. I am picking up the vibes that she's interested, but I'll wait and see where this will take me.

"Would you like a table?" she whispers, and I can hear the hope in her voice.

I lay my hand atop hers and squeeze; she sighs, and her luscious, red-painted lips part slightly, then turn up in a welcoming smile.

She tilts her head to one side and is about to speak again when a voice bellows from the kitchen area, "When you've finished with that customer, Ania, come here and take these plates."

And, just like that, the spell is broken.

She removes her hand from my arm and gives herself a little shake, placing her hands behind her back. She's in professional mode now. "Is there a table you would prefer?" she queries.

I'm not ready to let this little morsel go, not yet. I place my hand on her shoulder and can feel the heat rising from her body; she tries to move away from me, but can't. She raises her head and is mesmerised.

"I'm looking for a friend," I whisper softly, "He came in a few minutes ago and sat over there in the corner. Do you know where he is?"

She moves forwards, as though to fall into my arms, her beautiful eyes never leaving mine. "He left by the back door. His guest was waiting for him, and they left together."

I remove my hand from her shoulder and she groans; she's confused and a little dazed, unsure of what has just happened.

I ignore her distress. This mystery gets curiouser and curiouser. How interesting, as I hadn't seen anyone else at the table.

"What did the woman look like?" I ask.

"What woman? What are you talking about?" the girl answers, and she attempts to move away from me.

"My friend," I insist, "I was supposed to meet him, but I got caught in the people rush out there." I point to the esplanade, not turning to view it, but keeping eye contact with this precious bite.

"Um… um…"

"Take your time; when you're ready, will you describe the girl who was sitting at the table when my friend arrived?"

"Oh… oh, that lady. She was quite beautiful. She had black hair, lovely eyes and white skin, like alabaster. She looked afraid when her guest arrived; we were concerned for her, but she left with him, laughing and holding his hand. May I show you to a table now, sir?"

I step back, remove my contact, with regret, and a coldness settles inside me. "There's no need; I'd better go and find my friend, as he'll not be happy I was late." I turn to leave the restaurant when I feel a hand on my back. I look over my shoulder, and it is the hostess.

"You're going the wrong way," she explains, and removes a dark curl that had freed itself from her tight hairstyle and had fallen onto her forehead; she pulls it and tucks it behind her ear. "They went out the back door, and we saw them walking across to the steps that take them to Victoria Street." She points to where they had headed.

I touch her face and thank her, my eyes promising that we will meet again.

"Ania!" screams the chef, and, with that, she moves rapidly away from me, not looking back to see if I have stayed or left.

I leave the restaurant and wander down towards the Royal Mile; I'm interested in the tall man I'd seen and the woman he met, but I want to enjoy the sights of Edinburgh before becoming embroiled in another drama that's not of my making.

I walk along the cobbled road, the traffic is heavy heading along the George IV Bridge towards the Mound, so I cross and begin walking down the Royal Mile. I pass St Giles Church; it gives me the shivers. Then I reach the Tron Church, and I'm about to cross another road, one that the people of Edinburgh call "The Bridges"; I'm walking so slowly that I've almost stopped, because of the masses of people who have arrived for the festival. They bump and barge into me, and I must confess to becoming aggrieved with all of them. If I could sweep them away like skittles down the hill, I would, but I know that the little mistdreamer will find me, and Heaven only knows what he intends to do to me if I use power wrongly. I'll bide my time, use it sparingly, and know he won't find out if it's just a little magic now and again.

No cars are allowed to drive down the Royal Mile during the festival, and that's simply because the people are shoulder to shoulder, in their thousands. Whenever there's a break, it's because of street performers: men on stilts wearing ridiculous outfits, handing out leaflets to entice people to come to see their plays and performances; a musician here and there, drowned out by the sounds of talking; fire-eaters and jugglers; and singers and actors. The noise is giving me a headache. The crowding and pushing makes me feel sick, and it's just one person too many. I cannot hold my frustration in any longer and I just do it...

I just...

I point my finger at a performer – a man wearing a hairy wig, who I think is a Viking – and I touch his shoulder, popping him like I would a balloon. As his remains fall, they catch the legs of four people, who fall too, and, as they topple, they begin to roll down the hill bumping into more legs, who fall…

Another person, this time a woman who is dressed as – well, I have no idea what she is, but I object to the face paint – and so, pop, my finger bursts her as well. Down she goes and she rolls into three more people, who stumble and are not able to catch hold of anyone to prevent them hitting the ground.

It's positively joyful until panic erupts. There are too many people falling. Some are getting crushed.

A fleeting thought enters my mind, Should I help them? Would it be possible to save them from the carnage I've caused? I watch the scene ahead of me; it's chaos. I smirk for a moment, proud of my work, but then I bend to assist one of the fallen when something catches the back of my leg. Then it's my turn to fall, but, before the ground crashes into my face, a strong arm grabs me and pulls me up to stand firmly on the ground. I am about to thank my hero when I realise it's the tall man I had been following.

I can hardly believe it. It's Flauros, wearing a trench coat!

"Come with me quickly," he insists, and he pulls me out of harm's way, whilst shaking his head at the disaster I've just caused.

"Why are you here?" I push him in the chest, freeing myself from his grip. "How did you find me?"

"How we found you is of no import, but you have to return to Hell."

"Why?" I laugh. "Is all Hell breaking loose?" I laugh at my own cleverness, but stop when I note the horror on his face. "You're joking? My demons are breaking out? What are the dukes and kings doing about it?" Lord, this is so frustrating; I can't even have a vacation and trust them to act in my place.

"I escaped," Flauros says quietly as we walk in the opposite direction from my human skittles. "The kings and dukes have been captured, and they are now in your darkest pits and dungeons. You'll remember being put there yourself at the end of the Mistdreaming War?"

"Pardon?" What on earth is he talking about? "When was I put in the pits?"

"How is it you remember nothing of the war?" he asks incredulously. He scratches the back of his neck hard, then his hand moves to his forehead where he pushes his hair from his face. He sighs with obvious vexation.

I'm pacing back and forth, angry that my kingdom could be so disrupted and distraught that I have no knowledge of my part in the war.

"Could you not take care of the place for four days? I cannot believe it turns to chaos when I've not been away for even a week!" I storm.

Flauros is staring at me as though I'm in need of a psychiatrist, and I want to slap him.

"What..." I shout, "What is your problem and why are you hiding from me?"

"Sire..." He speaks to me as though I've lost my mind, which only intensifies my anger. "You have been gone for more than three of Earth's years."

That stops me in my tracks. "It's not possible... I came here four days ago..." I stop arguing with him, as I'm taken aback by his astonishment. There's no triangle on the ground, and it's clear he's telling the truth.

And that's when it dawns on me.

"That little shit," I shout.

"Sire, are you all right?" Flauros asks, concerned about me.

"That little mistdreamer forgot to tell me about the time lapse when I jumped through the years. I'm going to kill him!"

"That might not be such a good idea" Flauros insists, "I've brought someone with me to aid you in your bid to get home."

"Why do I need anyone else's help? How is it you cannot help me?"

Flauros wrings his hands nervously. "I escaped from Hell, narrowly avoiding death and without telling anyone where I would be; not even the angels are aware of my fall to Earth. I have no powers other than the ability to get myself back to our kingdom."

I let this bit of knowledge sink in; Flauros was proving to be my loyal servant, once more, and the friend I always knew he was. I relaxed and put myself in his hands. "Tell me then, who would this wise one be?"

"Once, a long time ago, she was a mermaid." When he becomes aware of my irrational fear, his hands make a calming gesture. "There's no need to fret about her; she has been a sea serpent for some time, and she has forgotten what it is like to be a mermaid. I believe she was also responsible for the deaths of many of her sisters, so her punishment was to remain as the dead."

"Why would she help me?" I enquire cynically. "Is it simply revenge?"

"There's an element of revenge, yes, but she has been promised her freedom if she aids you."

My mind is in a fog, and I try to work out what all of this means. I hear the screams behind me, as the melee is turning into a human tidal wave.

Flauros grabs my arm. "We must go quickly, before the mistdreamers find us."

I'm in agreement with him, and we walk up the Royal Mile until we reach the George IV Bridge. Taking a left turn, we walk past the library and the hotel opposite, until we turn right into Victoria Street.

That's when I see her. She is divine. The hostess didn't do this lady's appearance justice. I get a glimpse of her face before she turns away, obviously searching for us. Her black hair falls in soft curls down her back, almost reaching her waist. When she turns round, her eyes are open wide; is it fear I can see? She's definitely nervous. Her violet eyes – fringed with heavy, black eyelashes – are enormous, and she has a small nose, high cheekbones and wide, full, red lips. But what a body! She has curves in the right places and is not too tall; she's at least a foot smaller than me. She has large breasts, a small waist and legs that could go on forever! She's wearing tight jeans that show off her legs to perfection and a t-shirt that fits like a glove.

I am in love and totally entranced by this vision. I notice Flauros heading towards her purposefully and hold back to watch their greeting. Are they lovers? I feel an insane jealousy; if they are, I will kill him.

When he approaches her, he looks disdainfully at her, as though she is a rotten piece of meat and my concerns about their relationship are allayed. That's when Flauros realises I am no longer with him, but have stopped. His rapid gestures telling me to come forwards are an indication he is concerned. I stroll towards them and, yes, there it is: she's noticed me. She can't take her eyes from me, and it sends my heart racing. She likes what she sees.

"Nick, meet Nathaira." Flauros says her name with such distaste that I'm surprised at his lack of manners.,"Nathaira this is Nick."

I ignore him and lift her hand, kissing the back of it softly. The promise of what is to come between us is poured into that one small kiss.

Flauros pulls my hand away. I look at him angrily and note the tight lips and the flared nostrils; his eyebrows are lowered and his eyes glaring.

"What's your problem?" I ask.

"We don't have time for you to be fawning all over her," he hisses.

"If you dislike her so much, why have you chosen her to assist me?" I wonder.

"She's the one with the gift, and the knowledge of how and where it will be made possible. I can't even enter her domain, but she can take you there under a blanket of secrecy. Then she will lead you back to our world."

"What's in it for you, Nathaira?" I want to hear her answer, not the second-hand version I've got from Flauros.

Her voice washes over me like a warm summer breeze; it's enticing and mesmerising as it rises and falls with the lilt in her tones. "I want to be free of my father; I want to walk the land and die."

My eyes fly open, with the summer breeze turning to a winter chill. "Die?" I question, "Why do you want to die? There will be no more of you."

"If I die," she sings, "then I'm human, and I'm no longer a prisoner of the sea. I've paid my price for the sins I committed against my family, and I've been forgotten. If I die and I'm punished, then I will find myself in the right place when my spirit leaves my body, but at least I no longer will have a body, sitting on cold stone and keeping alive by eating molluscs."

"Then I hope you've been incredibly bad during the time you've become a human because I look forward to an eternal life with you by my side."

I don't see Flauros's hands shaking, but I notice he's shuffling his feet.

"What's the matter with you?" I shout at him.

"We have to go. Do you accept Nathaira's proposition?" he barks. "I can feel the mistdreamers nearby; you have to make a choice and do it quickly, or you might never get back."

I find it quite entertaining watching him getting into such a flap, but he's right; there's no need to delay. "I accept," I confirm.

And with those two simple words my life ends.

Twelve

"Where the hell is he?" shouted Omniel. He really should learn not to lose his temper because when he does, all sorts of problems erupt on Earth.

On this occasion, however, Ambriel was in total agreement. "How could we have lost him?" he asked. "We had him marked; the mistdreamer pinned him with the time spell we gave him, so we should have been able to track him easily."

"We did until he got to Edinburgh. We have to send someone there to find out what's going on," Omniel pushed. "Either that or we just send someone to Castle Moy to talk with the mistdreaming children."

"Who do you want to send?" enquired Ambriel.

"Our best bet would be to contact Xaphan. He's already at Mingary Castle, so he could go to Castle Moy and find out anything he can, then let the mistdreamer come to us and tell us what's been discovered."

"That makes more sense," Ambriel agreed, "rather than risking another angel getting lost."

"I can't believe it," Omniel fumed. "He's disappeared! How can the King of Hell just disappear?"

"You need to calm down," Ambriel said quietly, "you're causing volcanic eruptions all over Earth. Ones that are extinct are beginning to awaken. Calm down, Omniel!"

Omniel took a deep breath, tucked his wings behind him and sat down on one of the high-backed leather chairs in the solar room in Heaven.

"What are we to do?" he asked worriedly, "All Hell is breaking loose. I never would have believed the time would come when I would be grateful that Lucifer is the King of Hell. He has to get back there and sort out the mess he's caused by taking his damn vacation!"

"If you explode once more, there won't be a planet Earth," Ambriel yelled, "then he'll be lost forever. For our Father's sake, get a grip of your emotions!"

Omniel placed his head in his hands, frustration and fear taking control of him. He breathed evenly, out and in, to calm himself.

"That's better. Wait here whilst I contact Xaphan." Ambriel fell to the earth like a shooting star falling from the sky, and landed within Mingary Castle's courtyard.

The two mistdreaming children were play-fighting and stopped when they watched the ball hit the ground. Xaphan and Adramelechk prepared themselves to attack, their swords at the ready. When Ambriel materialised, they withdrew their swords and crossed the square to welcome him.

"It's been a while," declared Xaphan, "You'll be needing our help again, I take it?"

"Has this anything to do with that Nick person whom young Christopher met up with a few weeks ago?" asked Adramelechk.

Ambriel brushed the glittering stars away from his white cloak and extended his wings. "I don't bring good news, I fear. We have lost Nick and have no idea where he might be. Hell is going to break loose in three years' time." He turned and looked at Christopher. "That's the years we added when he went forwards in time, and he was mightily angry when he discovered our deception." He grinned with the boys, who were delighted that the plan they had suggested to Omniel had been put in place.

"Ah cud ask the mermaids," ventured Christopher.

"Ah dinnae think he'd go wi' them, Chris," his brother Paul said. "He's terrified o' them."

"It's not the mermaids," Ambriel explained, "but water he fears."

"Mebbe he didnae hae a choice and was taken there," Paul suggested.

"We had thought about that, but who would have the opportunity and the ability to get him to agree to go there?" enquired Ambriel.

The boys shook their heads from side to side and said in unison, "We dinnae ken."

One archangel and two ex-angels turned suddenly, and all of them stared at the little boys, who looked the very picture of innocence. All three together enquired, "What are you two not telling us?"

*

I am cold, wet and miserable. To top it all, I am beyond angry. When I'd agreed to the voluptuous beauty Nathaira's help, I'd fallen into a spellbound trap that was a contract of some sort, and I'd been carried away to Castle Moy.

I was uncertain if the mistdreamers were involved, but if they were, I intended to wreak havoc upon them and every other mistdreamer alive. Even if they weren't involved, it is my duty to end their lives, so – just for the fun of it – I intend to kill them. That, of course, will be when I'm free from this watery darkness I find myself trapped in.

I know that Flauros is the ringleader, and I had stupidly put my trust in him.

I'm going to kill him as well, or worse!

I'm sitting at the bottom of a well, which is in the circular building I'd seen built behind Castle Moy. The chieftain had spoken about its unknown depths, and I had tried to fathom out how accurate he had been. I'd only been able to dive so far before having to return to the surface.

I'm hungry, I hate water, it's dark, and if I'm being punished, what better way than to hold me in this prison?

"Do you hear me," the voice whispers.

I'm desperate for company, but I recognise her voice and refuse to answer; her betrayal will not go unpunished.

"I know you can hear me. I didn't want to do this to you; I was promised my life, but he lied. I'm sorry," she whispers. "I've brought you food."

A crab floats up from the depths, and I pull it apart, eating all of it and laying the shell on the ledge beside me. It could be used for a plate; I have to have some civility, even if it's in a deep well!

I'm surely going to be found soon, as my demons will search for me; I can wait…

*

"We warned him tae behave himsel'," Christopher answered, looking down at his foot, which was drawing circles in the earth.

"But we kenned he wudnae, so we spelled him," Paul interjected, his arms crossed against his chest.

Ambriel waited patiently for the rest of the information, his brows furrowed.

"We just spelled him tae come back here if he was naughty," Christopher said, looking up at the archangel.

"You believe him to be here?" asked Ambriel warily.

"Weeell, no' yet." Paul looked to Xaphan for help.

"No, don't do that; you did this." Xaphan shook his head, astonished that the five-year-old boys would arrange this by themselves and not tell him or Adramelechk. "You are responsible for the repercussions."

Christopher sniffed, as did Paul – both little boys refused to cry – then together they stared at Ambriel with determination.

"We dinnae ken where he is, but we ken when he is, though," explained Christopher.

"Ye can go forwards in time an' find him, can ye no'?" the boys asked in unison.

"Oh Lordy me." Ambriel fashioned a chair and plopped down in it. "You've really done it, boys. No, I can't go forwards in time, because the year he finds himself in is on a different timeline to the one we are on."

"So…" two little voices said together.

"So, if I go forwards on this timeline, I could change history. Many things might not happen that should happen," clarified Ambriel.

"Then change the timeline," Christopher stated reasonably.

"I could change that," replied Ambriel, shaking his head, "but if I do that, I could change the past; it could mean mistdreamers are never born. There are too many things in history that have fashioned this world, which might not happen."

"Oh," said Paul.

"Oh," Christopher repeated.

"Yes, 'oh,'" Ambriel added.

"What can we do?" Adramelechk stepped forwards and picked both boys up, holding one in each of his arms; he'd felt their discomfort and wouldn't allow anyone to cause them pain. He held onto them, and they put their arms around his neck and couried into his chest.

"We'll have to wait the three years out; I can't even make time move faster, because speeding up time might eliminate elements of great importance."

The little boys had been so brave and felt so guilty that, with this last piece of knowledge, both began to cry into Adramelechk's chest, their shoulders shaking as they sobbed.

Ambriel's heart went out to them; this was a problem, but not an insurmountable one. They knew what was going to happen, and they could be prepared for the demon insurrection. He would contact the dragons and get their support, together with every mystical being on Earth that would suffer when the hordes of Hell broke loose. "We will work this out, little men, but, in future, if you're going to cast a spell, tell Xaphan or Adramelechk first," he chastised.

They both nodded, still holding tightly to Adramelechk.

Christopher was the first to look over at Ambriel. "In three years, the mermaids will help us find him. They'll ken where he is."

Ambriel rose. "I must return to Heaven and tell Omniel; we will then get to work on a plan. I say to both of you, Xaphan and Adramelechk – be prepared. Keep these warriors safe." He tousled the boys' hair. "I must be gone, but we will be the victors, if all is put in place."

*

In the great throne room of Hell, Flauros sat upon the Conjurer's throne, tapping his nails on the large armrests. The angels would know by now what he had done, and they would be closing the gates to Hell soon. Until then, he had released several of his dukes and demons; their plan was in place and they would win this time.

There would be no interference from mistdreamers or any other angelic body.

This time the Earth would belong to Hell.

CPSIA information can be obtained
at www.ICGtesting.com
Printed in the USA
LVHW031103170320
650297LV00009B/482